STICKS AND STONES

A DCI HARRY MCNEIL NOVEL

JOHN CARSON

DCI SEAN BRACKEN SERIES

DI FRANK MILLER SERIES

Crash Point

Silent Marker

Rain Town

Watch Me Bleed

Broken Wheels

Sudden Death

Under the Knife

Trial and Error

Warning Sign

Cut Throat

Blood from a Stone

Time of Death

Frank Miller Crime Series – Books 1-3 – Box set

Frank Miller Crime Series - Books 4-6 - Box set

MAX DOYLE SERIES

SCOTT MARSHALL SERIES

Old Habits

STICKS AND STONES

ONE

It was the smell that hit him first. He'd read books where the detective said he smelled blood, but he had never smelled blood before. He wasn't even sure it was blood, but it was something strange.

He was aware of the silence next. The house was never this quiet. His sister was usually home from school and his mother would be in the kitchen making something for dinner.

Today there was nothing but silence. No smell of cooking, but something else entirely. Something that scared him.

His father's car was in front of the house. He thought maybe he'd got home early, but that in itself was unusual.

All three things scared him. The smell, the quiet

and his father's car. Those were the three things he would focus on in the years to come.

He wanted to call out to his mother but felt foolish. He was sure his voice would sound panicked like it would if he was a little boy instead of a teenager. What if they were out in the back garden? No, he would surely hear voices. All he could hear were birds outside.

He made his way to the stairs and stopped, listening for any sound from upstairs. Anything. A movement, somebody talking in hushed tones. A floorboard creaking. Anything. But he heard nothing.

He took the first step, his heart starting to beat faster now. He wouldn't have been so worried if it wasn't for the smell. He didn't *want* to go upstairs, but he felt he *had* to. There was no way of getting around this.

He took another step and stopped as the tread creaked under his weight. He knew which stairs made a noise, but he hadn't been thinking about that. Now he did, careful where he placed each foot as he climbed higher.

He turned on the small landing where the next set of stairs were, heading higher up in the opposite direction of the first set. Stairs he had climbed thousands of times before, but which now seemed like he was climbing for the first time, not knowing it was going to be the last time.

The house was big and isolated.

He reached the main landing, the smell getting worse.

A short hallway faced the stairs. A door on the left led into the bathroom, the opposite door into his bedroom. The other hallway ran left to right, with three other doors; his mum and dad's bedroom, his sister's bedroom and the spare room for Uncle Jack, when he had been out drinking with dad and was too drunk to drive home.

He took the right, along to his sister's room. There was a window at the end of the hallway, throwing some light onto the carpet. There was also light coming from Maggie's room. He walked slowly after looking along the other end of the hallway. Both doors were closed there. His parents' room and the spare.

He walked towards Maggie's room. He remembered looking down at the pattern, a gold colour spun through the deep red.

Deep red. Just like blood.

He tried to call out his sister's name, but his voice was just a croak. His mouth was dry and he couldn't get his tongue to move. His legs felt like solid logs of wood that wouldn't move properly, just like the time he

3

had a dream that the house was on fire and he couldn't run out, no matter how hard he tried.

He willed himself to move forward, feeling the icy grip of terror. He didn't know why. Couldn't explain it to himself.

The smell.

It was close.

He stood outside Maggie's room. His mother told him he always had to knock before entering her room, but the door was wide open. He took a few breaths, in through the nose, out through the mouth.

Then he stepped in front of the doorway.

The room was empty.

Her soft toys were on the bed. Their mother always made their beds early in the day. She said if she accomplished that simple task, it set her up for the rest of the day.

He turned away and walked towards the other end of the hallway, his legs starting to move faster, like an old engine will cough into life and start running normally.

He almost felt relief after seeing his sister's room empty. It was like there was nothing wrong at all.

Except for the smell, which was getting stronger.

His parents' room was on the left. A window was set in the wall at the far end, just like the one outside Maggie's room.

That's why he didn't see the sliver of light falling from the doorway. The bedroom door was ajar. The door to the spare room over on his right was closed. This door was open. Where the smell was thickest.

He always had to knock on this door too, if it was closed.

But it was open.

The hinges creaked ever so slightly as he slowly pushed the door open wider. It was a different carpet in here. Beige with no patterns. He was looking down at it, not wanting to lift his eyes. Then he saw the new pattern on the carpet.

Little red circles. Different sizes. Not near the door but closer to the back wall. He lifted his head, his eyes slowly looking at the wallpaper. It too had the same pattern on it.

Little red circles. Big red circles.

As he opened the door wider, he saw the big red circles became something else entirely. Big patterns, with something else mixed in.

No matter how many times he thought about what he saw next, the thing he focused on first was his sister's eyes. Looking at him. Looking *through* him.

She was sitting on the bed, facing him. Behind her lay the cooling corpse of their mother. Where her head had been was now a bloody mess. He looked at Maggie, wordlessly begging for her to give him the answer, but she just sat silently.

He couldn't breathe. He tried drawing a breath but only succeeded in little pockets of air hitting his lungs.

He stood rooted to the spot when he felt the hairs on the back of his neck stand up. It was the tiniest of sounds, barely audible, a sound he wouldn't have heard if there had been any other ambient noise in the house, but he heard the noise and he felt the kind of fear he had never before experienced in his young life.

He couldn't move, couldn't turn round to see what the noise was. There was nowhere for him to run to even if he had turned round.

Then he felt the barrels of the shotgun placed against the back of his head.

'Sit on the bed beside your sister,' his father said, but it didn't sound like his father. His voice was rough and dry.

He couldn't move at first, but then the gun was pressed harder against his head and he felt himself step forward on shaky legs. He tried not to look at his sister or what was left of his mother. His sister stirred slightly as he sat down on the mattress.

His father kept the gun pointed at him as he slowly walked into the room.

'Please, Dad, don't do this,' he said, his voice cracked and broken.

His father sat down in a chair in the corner of the room, the one that his mother used to sit in and read.

He could feel his body tensing, waiting for the buckshot that would kill him.

The buckshot that would create more little red circles.

He wanted to get up and run but his legs had stopped working. He just sat and waited to die.

But his father didn't kill him.

'Tell them it wasn't me,' his father said, his voice low, barely above a whisper.

He turned the shotgun, which the boy saw had been shortened, and put it under his chin.

He jumped a little as the noise of the gun reverberated around the room. Maggie sat staring.

He sat looking as his dead father now lay slumped in the chair. It would be a full hour before he could find the ability to move.

His father's words echoed through his head. *Tell them it wasn't me*. But it *was* him. Who else could have killed his mother?

It was only years later that the true meaning of his father's words would sink in.

But by then, it was too late.

TWO

'You can't hide behind those sunglasses for ever,' DS Alex Maxwell said, dropping a gear in her BMW and flooring it.

'For the last time, my eyes are not bloodshot. I'm just tired, that's all.' DCI Harry McNeil reclined the seat a bit more after being thrown back into it. Usually Sunday morning was for sobering up, not heading north out of Edinburgh with a member of his Major Investigation Team.

'None of my business what you get up to in your own time,' Alex said.

'Correct.' He fidgeted in the seat, trying to get more comfortable. 'We could have taken a pool car, you know.'

'A manky Vauxhall that smells like a dog's been in it? No thanks.'

Alex hit the outside lane on the Queensferry Crossing bridge and zipped past a long line of cars, trucks and weekend warriors towing caravans.

Harry closed his eyes and recalled snatches of the conversation he'd had with Ness that morning. They'd broken up a week ago, and she had wanted to meet for a talk. First were words of disbelief that Harry was being pulled into his office at HQ, then a suggestion that he might want to tell his boss to send him up north with DC Simon Gregg, and she had refused to listen to the fact that he had to be travelling with a DS and that meant Alex Maxwell. It wasn't his decision, but it came with the job.

Her reply inferred he should check his own colon later, where he'd find his job residing.

'What did Vanessa say when you told her you were travelling with me and we'll be there for at least an overnight stay?' Alex said, as if reading his mind.

'Never you mind. Just keep your eyes on the road and slow down. I don't want the fire brigade to be called out to something that isn't a drill.'

'You're tetchy today. Are you not enjoying your drive out into the country with your favourite DS?'

'You're my only DS. And no, I'm not. I just wish the high heid yins had given us a little more warning.'

Alex slowed the car down a bit for *Grandpa Harry.* 'She only went missing last night.'

9

Harry made a noise. 'Pedantics. Saturday night is for having a sociable beer and Sunday morning is for recovering from said sociable beer. Not reining it in just in case there's a phone call on the Sunday morning.'

'Must have been a riot, having a drink with Vanessa at the bowling club.'

'We do okay. The prices are cheap, that's why we go. They practically promote alcoholism.' He reached over and fiddled with the radio. 'Why do they have to make trannies so difficult to use nowadays?'

'Tranny?' Alex grinned at him.

'Short for transistor radio. My dad used the term. It stuck.' He found Radio 2.

'Good Lord, how old are you?' she said, about to reach over and change the station when he gently slapped her hand away.

'This might be your car, sergeant, but I've just commandeered it.'

'Yeah, right. I'll just change it back when you fall asleep. And by the look of you, you're not far off it.'

Harry yawned, reinforcing her opinion.

'Okay, have it your way. But since I have my sunglasses on, you won't know when my eyes are closed.'

'You don't snore, then?'

'See? This is why I would have chosen to drive up on my own. Peace and quiet and no lectures.'

'Apart from the fact you're hungover and would fail a breath test?'

'Touché.'

A few minutes later, the snoring and head tilt indicated that Harry's life might be in danger should Alex Maxwell decide that enough was enough, but she did nothing more dangerous than change the radio station.

Reaching Pitlochry they had a quick pitstop and a pie out of the bakery. Two for Harry.

'I'm a growing boy,' he said, squeezing by a tourist with a backpack on.

'Growing sideways though, eh?' Alex said with a grin.

They got back in the car and drove to a car park in the north part of town, next to where the buses and coaches parked. The sun was out bathing them in a welcome heat and they headed over to a small gazebo on the edge of the car park and sat at a little table.

'You know, another time, another life, this would be quite nice. You and me taking a drive up here. This is God's own country. I used to come up here with my mum and dad when I was wee. And my younger sister. You ever seen the Salmon Ladder?' Alex said, taking a bite out of her pie.

'Aye, a few times. I brought my son, Chance, up here a couple of times. We went camping, pitching a tent in the caravan park just up there, on the edge of town.'

'How did that go?' Alex asked, finishing her pie and wishing she had got a doughnut as well. She washed it down with a bottle of Coke.

'It was great. Just the two of us, sleeping in the tent, doing a little bit of fishing. Some hiking.'

'What about Vanessa? Does she like camping?'

'Unless it's got a bar and an en suite, she doesn't even entertain the idea of camping. *Glamping* she says she would do, but I'm sure that involves an expensive hotel instead of sleeping under the stars.'

'I wouldn't mind camping. I've done it before. When me and my mate went to *T in the Park*.'

'It's hardly the same thing, lying in a manky old tent, trying not to get trampled on, puking into a carrier bag.'

Alex nodded. 'Aye, it was a load of shite. People get raped. I would have stabbed some bastard before he got his hands on me. That's why I stayed sober, so I could look after my mate. She made drinking like a competition.'

'These things can be a magnet for deviants, right enough,' Harry said. 'Present company excepted.' He took the second pie out of the bag and bit into it.

'The diet starts tomorrow, eh?' Alex said.

'You're not going to make me feel guilty,' he said between mouthfuls. 'And Harry doesn't share.'

'As long as you wipe your greasy fingers before getting back into Betty.'

Harry looked at her, his eyebrows raised.

'My car; *Betty the blue Beemer* I call her.'

'Of course you do,' he replied, finishing the pie and scrunching up the paper bag.

Harry made a show of wiping his fingers with the paper napkin before putting his rubbish in the bin.

'With the wipes I keep in Betty, I meant.'

'See? I wouldn't have had to wipe my fingers this much with a pool car.'

'I know. A greasy pie would have improved the interior.'

'I'll give my hands an extra good wash,' he said, getting up and going over to the toilets.

With his hands thoroughly cleaned, they set off north again, catching the A9 past the campsite where Harry had taken Chance. It brought back a lot of good memories, and he hoped his son wasn't being misled by his mother and the band of gypsies she called a family.

A tune by U2 came on and Harry felt his foot tapping as Alex expertly guided her car up the road.

'You like 80s music, then?' she asked him.

'I do,' he said quietly, his mind slipping to a club he'd been in, many moons ago, with a woman he had spent the night with and had never seen again. He remembered this particular U2 song being played; *With or Without You.* He had gone home in the early hours of the morning, Morag already having moved out with Chance, and Harry had sat on the couch listening to music and slowly drinking himself into a stupor.

'You okay there, Harry?' Alex said, looking over to him for a moment.

He nodded, feeling far from okay. He had messed up one marriage, and now he was about to add a failed relationship to the pot. He closed his eyes and ran little private movies in his mind as the car drove north.

He must have dozed off because the next thing he knew, they were on the approach to Inverness, about to bypass it and cross over the Kessock Bridge.

'You ever been to Inverness before?' Alex asked.

She was either very good at bluffing or she didn't know much about him.

'I was born here,' he said.

'Really?' she replied, taking her eyes off the road for a moment. 'How did you end up working down the road for the Edinburgh police?'

'My grandmother was born in Fort George, in Ardersier, just over there,' he replied, pointing east of Inverness, 'a couple of years before the war, when the fort still had an infirmary. The family stayed up here, until 1991 when I was twelve. We moved down to

Kirkcaldy to live when my dad got a transfer from the police up here down to Fife.'

'Your dad was a copper too?'

Harry nodded. 'He was. He's dead now. The drink got to him. It ruined his marriage, and my parents divorced.'

'Were you ever in the Fife police?'

'No. I went to Edinburgh uni, but I was bored out of my crust. On a whim, I joined Lothian and Borders. And the rest is history.'

'And now you're coming home.' Alex looked at him as they crossed the bridge.

It took them less than an hour to make it the rest of the way to Dornoch, and five minutes from there to the Castle hotel just outside the small town.

And that's when the view of rolling hills became a sea of police vehicles parked on the road with a uniform standing in the middle with his hand up. Another walked about with a German Shepherd that looked like it hadn't had a good meal in days and any old arse would do to sink its teeth into.

A man in a suit walked over, smiling. 'Never mind that, son. They're the Edinburgh contingent.'

The uniform walked away with a quick glance back as if he didn't believe the man in the suit.

Dunbar bent down to look through the window.

'DS Alex Maxwell, meet DCI Jimmy Dunbar.

He's from Glasgow. The rougher version of Edinburgh,' Harry said.

'Pleased to meet you, sir.'

'Likewise, sergeant. Now, if my own sergeant would stop disappearing, I would be able to introduce him.' He looked at Harry. 'Better watch what I say. Considering there's a lassie missing.'

'Aye, that kind of talk might upset the natives.'

'It's no' them I'm worried about upsetting, Harry; it's her old man. And the groom's father. Although the bride's mother's a bit of a Rottweiler too. Looks like his trophy wife. Come on, I was just getting the team together. I want a briefing before we go any further. Follow me.'

He walked away and got into a car and they tailed him through the gates and down the road towards the castle itself.

'He's the lead investigator?' Alex asked.

'He has seniority.' Harry looked at her. 'Look on the bright side; if the bride finally does decide to come back, they have a spa.'

'Not my style, sir. Not my style at all.'

'I forgot. Boggin old tents and pishing in a bucket for you.'

'Don't knock it 'til you've tried it.'

'I've had the tee shirt that long, it's faded.'

As they got closer to the castle itself, Harry could

see more police vehicles parked outside the front door. And he got a bad feeling. This was just too much activity for somebody who was only listed as missing.

Then he saw the bride's father striding over to DCI Dunbar's car and shouting at the detective as he got out of his car.

'What's his problem?' Alex said.

'He's the bride's father. Broderick Gallagher. You'll see why he's got a problem.'

They got out of the car into the cooler north air and the man turned and came towards them.

THREE

'Are you the Edinburgh crowd?' Broderick Gallagher said, now rounding on Harry. The man was in his fifties, and he was well built, with a red face that suggested he might be in need of the hotel's defibrillator shortly.

'DCI Harry McNeil, Edinburgh MIT. This is DS—'

'Never mind her,' Gallagher said, dismissing the lower ranks. 'I want to know what the hell you're going to do about my daughter. It's been well over twelve hours since she went missing! On her wedding night, no less!'

'That's why we've been sent up here, to backup Inverness MIT, sir. If you could let us inside, we'll get an update then talk to you all. We're just as keen to find her as—'

'Bollocks. Just get on with it. Bloody well do something.' Gallagher strode away. Harry looked over at Dunbar who was resisting the temptation to add Gallagher to the missing person's list.

'He's a charmer,' Alex said as they made their way into the hotel with Dunbar.

'He's a very rich charmer,' Harry said.

'We've taken over the library,' Dunbar said, seeing his DS poke his head out for a moment before disappearing back inside.

They went in and saw a whiteboard set up, and people being interviewed at the far end by men in suits.

'That's the Inverness lot,' the young sergeant said, coming over to them. 'The old school.'

'That's enough, Robbie,' Dunbar said. 'We're here to help them not take the piss.' He looked at Harry and Alex. 'This is DS Robert Evans.'

Harry acknowledged the younger man. Boaby by name, boaby by nature. He'd seen many like him before, and all of them had crashed and burned. No doubt Evans would be the same one day.

'Right, let's get a seat and see what's going on,' he said to Dunbar. 'We were told only the basics and that you would fill us in when we got here.' He was about to add *sir* when he remembered he too was a DCI. The promotion had only kicked in a few weeks earlier and he was still getting used to it.

The four detectives sat at a table. 'Tell me what you know, Harry,' Dunbar said.

'I got a call first thing this morning telling me that a young bride had gone missing up here. Her father is Broderick Gallagher, owner of our local newspapers, *The Caledonian* and *The Edinburgh Evening Post.*'

'Aye, and she just married into the Randall family, from our neck of the woods. Terence Randall, head of the Randall car empire. It's his son who got hitched to Marie Gallagher.'

'Both families are multi-millionaires, I assume,' Alex said, 'or else we wouldn't be here for a missing person.'

'You assume correctly, sergeant,' Dunbar said. 'That's why there's a lot of squawking, and why the chief constable got a phone call late last night. And pish runs downhill. I was given a quick briefing and sent up here with this young reprobate. And told to pack a suitcase.'

'I was much the same. Not that DS Maxwell's a reprobate, you understand,' he added, when he saw Alex looking at him.

'Well this clown is.' He looked at Evans as if expecting an argument and getting none.

'What's the latest report?' Harry asked.

'Still the same as earlier. They have uniforms out scouring the grounds, along with dog handlers and the stewards who work here. Butlers with kilts.'

'This is a big place, then?'

Dunbar chuffed. 'Big? It's twenty thousand acres. There are lodges over the other side of the river that splits this place.' They also bought land to the north and an old, run-down estate to the west. The properties all border each other. We've been given a room each to stay in while we're here.'

'At the very least, she'll turn up and we can have a wee sesh then head back down the road,' Harry said.

'Maybe they had a fight, nobody knew about it and she decided to play silly buggers,' Alex said.

'We asked the guests and staff, but none have said they heard anything like that. We're still working our way through them.'

Harry looked at a man who had approached them. He was one of a few he had seen walking about; dressed in a tweed jacket and kilt, with a bunnet. He had a well-trimmed bushy beard.

'My name is Angus McPhee, the head steward. Can I get you folks anything? Soft drink, perhaps?'

Harry was sweating and nodded that he would indeed like a drink. 'Yes, please. I'd like a water.'

'I'll get one of my men to bring some over. A few of them are being interviewed just now.'

'How about you?' Harry said. 'You been interviewed already?'

'I was the first one, sir.' His voice was rough Scottish, and there was a hardness in the man's eyes that belied his smile.

'Good. I'll want to talk to you myself, just to be brought up to speed. My name's DCI McNeil from Edinburgh.'

'Well, DCI McNeil from Edinburgh, I'll go and get those drinks organised.'

They watched the big man walk away.

'I'd like to talk to the parents,' Harry said.

'They're through in the big lounge,' Dunbar said. 'Broderick and Anne Gallagher. They've been spoken to by Inverness, but I told them we'd want to talk to them as well. They weren't happy but if they want help in finding their daughter, they better get the pokers out of their arses first. We'll talk to them and I'll introduce you to the Inverness team leader. A young DI. He looks sound as a pound but time will tell.'

Harry looked over to the other side of the room where Dunbar indicated and saw a man in his thirties, busy talking to what looked like a couple of guests.

One of the stewards came over with glasses of soft drinks. Harry took his water and gulped half of it back.

'You should have got a hair of the dog,' Alex said in a low voice.

'Behave. It's just warm outside.'

'Right, let's go over and set the room on fire.' Dunbar said and they marched across the wide reception hall. Harry could imagine how this would have looked as a private castle many years ago, the men coming back from fighting whoever it was they fought back then.

The only clans in the big room now were the two families; one from Glasgow, the other from Edinburgh. They sat on chairs and couches in different parts of the large room, as if waiting to go into battle.

By the looks of things, some of them already had.

'Any news?' a woman said, standing up. The bride's mother, Harry assumed, after Dunbar's less than flattering description of her. She was nothing like a Rottweiler. She was Broderick Gallagher's trophy wife, and had he not been told that, he might have thought she was one of his daughters. Her eyes were red but had a shiny look to them as if she were ready for a fight.

'We've only just arrived from Edinburgh,' Harry said, turning to look at Alex briefly. 'I'm DCI Harry McNeil and this is DS Alex Maxwell. We'd like to talk to you and your family, if we could. Perhaps in another room?'

The woman turned to her husband and Gallagher looked at her as if prepared for a stand-off but then his shoulders slumped and he followed her. Harry watched them until they left the room before speaking to Dunbar.

'Where's the groom?'

'Floating about somewhere. He was out with one of the search parties earlier. He broke down when I told him we'd have to get the underwater team out. There's a small lake and the river to consider.'

'Right. What about the Glasgow side?'

'I'll have a chat with them then we can compare notes.'

Harry indicated for Alex to follow him, and back outside in the grand hall, he just caught a glimpse of Broderick Gallagher slipping through a doorway. Considering there were a lot of people floating about, Harry thought the man an ignoramus. He was getting all the help he needed in trying to track his daughter down, yet here he was swanning about with complete disregard for the people who were helping him.

The room was a library. It was stuffy, with the kind of smell that old library books had. He wished he'd brought the water in with him.

'How the hell can she just disappear from here?' Gallagher said, rounding on Harry, but Harry had been in a room with many more dangerous people than this man, been threatened with worse, been attacked and this outburst didn't come close to anything like fazing him.

'Sit down, Mr Gallagher,' Harry said, taking a seat. Alex sat close by.

Gallagher wasn't used to being spoken to like that and his jaw moved up and down for a few seconds, before his wife put a hand on his arm and he took a seat.

'I want you to run through the events of last night, leading up to your daughter going missing, then what happened after you discovered she was gone.'

They locked eyes for a moment, but once again, Harry knew that Gallagher didn't even come close to any of the people he'd had to deal with when he was with Professional Standards, investigating other police officers.

'The wedding was splendid, of course. It went without a hitch and then we had the dinner. In the banquet hall. It was superb. Marie was so happy. *We* were both happy.' He looked at his wife. Anne Gallagher nodded, confirming that – although it wasn't on the same level as a Caligula family gathering – they had indeed had a good time.

'Then after Marie and Duncan danced, it was announced that the couple were going upstairs to get changed and would be back down. Nobody thought anything of it. Yes, she was taking her time, but she had a big wedding dress to get out of.'

'Was anybody in the room with her?' Alex asked. 'Helping her to get out of her dress.'

'Yes. Claire, her chief bridesmaid. Duncan was in his own room with his best man, Laurence. He wanted to give him the gift he'd bought. An inscribed silver tankard. They had a couple of whiskies, then they went along to Marie's room and Claire came out. Marie said she would be down shortly after that. The three of them came back down to the reception room where the dancing was in full swing, leaving Marie alone in the room.'

'He went up with her and came back down without seeing anyone else?'

'Yes. Laurence and Claire were with them all the way, and never saw anybody else.'

Harry pictured the scene in his mind. 'Are there cameras in the hotel?'

'Yes. Although it turns out, the one in that hallway isn't working. There's a gatehouse that's closed at night and there are always stewards on throughout the night in case a guest wants something. Security was a big reason for having the wedding here.'

Alex looked at him. 'Between the time they went upstairs, and somebody going to look for Marie, what time span are we looking at?'

Gallagher looked at his shoes as if the answer lay in the carpet.

His wife answered for him. 'A little over an hour. Close to ninety minutes, maybe.' She sounded more like a poodle than a Rottweiler now, Harry thought.

'Who first realised that she hadn't come back down?'

Anne Gallagher's lip trembled. 'Look, she was going to get changed into a simple dress. Something she could dance in. Then later on, she and Duncan were going to head up to the honeymoon suite before the dancing stopped around midnight.'

'What time did they go upstairs to get changed?'

'About eight thirty or so. It was around ten when somebody noticed she was taking ages. Duncan was already down here, mingling with the guests and you know what it's like; time gets away from you when you're having a good time.'

Harry looked at the father for a moment. 'Do you know if Marie was having any problems with anybody?'

'Not to my knowledge, she wasn't,' Anne said.

Harry looked at Gallagher, waiting for an answer.

'Mr Gallagher?'

'I'm a businessman. In my game, you don't get to the top without stepping on people. Of course I've had threats but didn't take anything seriously.'

'Bodyguards?' Alex asked.

'No bodyguards. Marie lived in her own place in the New Town in Edinburgh. Duncan had moved in with her. Much to his father's chagrin. He had suggested them moving through to Bearsden, but Marie was having none of it. She's in line to take over my newspapers and head up other business interests of mine. Duncan's family own dealerships through in Edinburgh as well as Glasgow, and he was already a dealer principle for their Lamborghini dealership, so they were both settled. But to answer your question, I never had a direct threat against my daughter.'

Anne started to cry and Gallagher put his arm around his wife's shoulders.

'We'll want to have a look at the room that Marie was last known to have been in,' Harry said. 'And Duncan's.'

'My head steward will show you,' Gallagher replied.

'Your steward?'

'Well, technically mine and Terry Randall's. Me and Terry bought this place six months ago. We own the hotel now.'

'I didn't realise.'

'Aye, it was too good an opportunity to pass up. It came on the market and I remembered the place from when we were making wedding plans. My Marie had talked about having her wedding here but it was fully booked. The original plan was to have it at some place in Edinburgh but we bought the place and since it was under new ownership, we reserved the right to cancel somebody's wedding plans.'

Harry looked at him.

'What, inspector? Don't look at me like that, just because I rained on somebody's parade. The lassie who was having her wedding here was well compensated. In fact, I picked up the tab for her wedding.'

'Just so your daughter could have her own wedding here?'

'It's just business. My Marie wanted this place and she got it. Besides, me and Terry saw what a good deal this place was. We're really going to put it on the map.'

'Marie didn't have problems with anybody, then?' Harry said. *Except maybe a family who had paid a hefty deposit for a daughter's wedding before it got the rug pulled out from under it.*

'Not that I can think of. I want your lot on top of this, McNeil; that's our home town. I don't want some... Inverness clodhopper missing something.'

'I'll get onto it.' Harry stood up. 'We still have a lot of people to talk to and it's going to be dark in a little while.'

Alex stood up as well. 'We'll do everything humanly possible to find out what happened to Marie.'

The parents just looked at the detectives as they left the room.

Harry turned to Alex. 'What's your gut instinct?'

She stopped and looked at him, waiting for a couple of stewards to walk past first before answering. 'Somebody took her and now's she dead.'

FOUR

'Aye, it's a strange one, alright,' Jimmy Dunbar said when he came out of one of the other rooms.

'How are the Randall family taking it?' Harry asked.

'The mother is up to high doh, but old man Randall seems more pissed off than anything, though trying not to show it.'

'What has Duncan Randall got to say for himself?' Alex asked.

'Nothing yet that I know of; he's away out on one of the searches again.'

'I think we should talk to the head steward,' Harry said. 'Any idea where he is?'

Dunbar looked over his shoulder. 'Skarting about somewhere. Probably pissing himself in case his job goes south and him along with it.'

'You heard about Gallagher and Randall being the new owners of this place?'

Dunbar lowered his voice a bit. 'I did. Randall's proud that he kicked some poor lassie's wedding into touch so his son could get married here yesterday.'

'Gallagher told me he took care of that wedding too though, to make up for it.'

'Maybe, but what if one of the other party got his hackles up about being pushed around? I'll have one of the Inverness boys check it out. The lassie was local. Her family are minted but even so, one of them might have spent all Friday night festering.' He looked at Evans. 'Get onto it, Sergeant Evans.'

Evans walked away and headed into the big ballroom where the Inverness boys were still conducting interviews.

'I'm hoping this is all a false alarm and we can spend the rest of the night getting pished in the bar,' Dunbar said.

'You and me both. But listen, I told Gallagher that I wanted to have a squint at the room where she was last seen.'

'Do that. I'll see if anybody remembers anything from last night, now that they've all sobered up.'

'Is her wedding dress in there, or did she have it on when she disappeared?'

'I spoke to the head of forensics, and the dress is gone.'

'That seems a bit strange. Her chief bridesmaid was in there with her, helping her get changed. I wonder where it's gone?'

'It might be something or nothing. I'll catch up with you,' Dunbar said, walking away.

Harry caught the head steward again, Angus McPhee. 'Can you show us the room where the missing woman was going to get changed? We can't find the manager.'

'I certainly can, sir. If you follow me up this staircase.'

The staircase itself ran up one side of the reception area. Covered in a plush tartan carpet, the walls were adorned with swords and animal heads, and paintings of men from a long time ago.

'You mind if I ask you a few questions?' Harry said, walking by the man's side. He was taller than Harry, who was a little over six feet himself. But that's where the similarity ended.

McPhee was big built with broad shoulders and looked like he tossed a few cabers before having his porridge for breakfast.

'Were you a military guy?' Harry asked as they reached the landing, Alex right behind them.

'Aye. How did ye know?'

'Just a guess.'

'You an army man?'

Harry shook his head. 'My brother was. He jumped out of planes for a living.'

McPhee smiled. 'Those are tough boys, let me tell ye. I was infantry myself. Nothing different from having a fight in the pub on a Friday night, except we got paid to do it and wear a uniform.' He smiled again and stopped outside a door.

Another man in a kilt and tweed jacket appeared at the other end of the corridor. Like a smaller version of McPhee. 'Sir, we're about to go on another search.'

'Carry on without me just now. I'm showing people around. My Land Rover's down there. Nobody take it and I'll catch up with you.'

'Aye, sir.' He disappeared through the door again.

'In here, sir,' McPhee said, opening the door and standing aside to let Harry and Alex in.

'Put your eyes back in your head, sergeant,' Harry whispered to Alex.

'How dare you.' She gave him the briefest of smiles before McPhee came into the room behind them.

'This is where the brides get changed before going back downstairs. Those who want to, of course. Not all of them do. But for those who do want, then this is the room. Where Marie was last seen.'

'Her husband confirmed he saw her coming in

here. He was with his friend and they collaborate each other's story,' Harry said, then turned to the big man. 'As well as the bridesmaid, of course. But she left. Could anybody have been waiting in here? Somebody who somehow got in who shouldn't be in here?'

McPhee's face darkened slightly, as if Harry had made a personal slight on his character. 'Not on my watch.'

'How would the bride access the room?' Alex asked.

'Like everybody gets into the rooms; the key is waiting behind reception. It isn't locked just now because they had a big dog in here earlier but there has to be the smell of a thousand guests in here, not to mention the staff. Then, as you can see, they had people with wee brushes going about putting powder everywhere.'

'Crime scene staff,' Harry said, like he was talking to somebody from another planet who had never watched TV before.

'Aye, them. But let me ask you; why all the activity? I mean, the poor woman is missing, but there have been people up here in the Highlands gone missing before and nobody bothered to lift an arse cheek off a seat. Now there's coppers from all over up here.'

'If you were a millionaire, wouldn't you want everything to be done to find your daughter?'

'I would want that even if I wasn't a millionaire.'

Harry thought the man had a fair point. He walked over to the window and looked down. There was no visible means of escape from the room, should a fire suddenly break out round the doorway, so it was safe to say Marie hadn't slipped out here and shimmied down a drainpipe.

'This whole place is around twenty thousand acres, isn't that right?' Harry said.

'Aye. It's a big estate, but it's a working estate. This estate was joined with two adjoining estates. It's going to be a big complex when they're finished. People come from all over the world to hunt and fish here while the women folk head off to the spa. Not all the women, like, but a gid few of them. Some of them like to have a go with the guns and they're pretty damned good.'

'They shoot ducks?' Alex said.

McPhee looked at her for a moment to see if she was playing with him, but then saw she was serious.

'Grouse. And clay pigeons of course.'

'There are lodges in the grounds,' Harry said, throwing Alex a look. *Ducks.* He looked around the room without touching anything.

'Yes. We service the lodges too, myself and the other stewards. We have twenty-five main lodges, which are basically houses, and then there's the rustic lodges, which are cabins, further into the woods.'

'And they're all occupied at the moment?' Alex asked.

Every one of them except a couple of the cabins, which have been made available to some of the police who have come up here. But rest assured, every one of them has been searched, and they were given the all clear.'

'Not much chance of her hiding in any of them while they're occupied, is there?' Harry said.

'No, sir. And the empty ones were searched more than once and they'll be occupied tonight.' He looked at his watch. 'I really need to go, sir. My men are doing another search in the grounds and in the woods and it's going to be dark soon.'

'That's fine. Off you go. Thanks for your help.'

McPhee left, leaving the door open, like he didn't trust them not to steal the family silver.

Harry looked at Alex. 'Marie comes in here, gets out of her wedding dress, packs it away, then just walks out after getting changed, taking her dress with her.'

'That about sums it up.'

'Why though? There is zero motive for her to do that. Unless...'

'Unless?'

'First of all, discounting your thoughts about somebody taking her and killing her, what if she had a secret lover and she ran away with him?'

'You mean, after taking her vows, and not before?'

'Aye, I do mean that. Stranger things have happened. What if she staged it this way? Make it look like she was happily married to her new husband, and she just vanishes.'

'She would have to be pretty messed up in the head to do that.'

'Alternatively, somebody was waiting for her to come here to the room. Somebody who was confident of being here without being questioned.'

'Duncan, her husband?'

'He could be standing outside here naked and nobody would ask him why he was loitering. They would just assume that he was waiting for her.'

Alex looked sceptical. 'His best man was with him.'

'I know they were in Duncan's room, but did the best man leave at any time before Duncan got changed? They were together but did either man leave the room at any time alone?'

'Damn. We should have asked McPhee before he left. Maybe he would have known.'

'Let's do one better; let's ask the men themselves, Duncan and his friend. Separately. And let's not give them a heads-up we're doing it. I'll talk to Dunbar about it.'

FIVE

Harry looked at his watch as they arrived in the main reception area again.

'Have you ever had that feeling that you're so hungry you could eat anything on legs?' Alex said.

'No.'

'Me neither. Although I am a bit peckish. It's past dinnertime.'

'You should have had two pies like me,' Harry said, giving her a look that said having two pies was a no-brainer.

'I'm thinking of eating healthier.'

'Weren't you thinking about it last week, too?'

'Thinking and doing are two different things.'

'Clearly.' Harry walked towards Dunbar who was talking to a younger man who had obviously given up the fight with his thinning hair a long time ago and who was on the fence about either shaving his head or going for a combover.

'Harry, this is DI Barrett. He's in charge of the Inverness team.'

'Good to meet you, sir,' Barrett said, looking at Alex.

'Likewise. This is DS Alex Maxwell.'

Barrett nodded to her, acting like he'd never spoken to a woman before.

'I'd like to speak to the best man and his friend,' Harry said. 'And the head bridesmaid.'

'We have them in the ballroom, waiting for you.'

'Lead the way.'

They started walking towards the back of the reception area and through a set of double doors, guarded by two uniforms, just in case any of the guests decided to make a run for it.

The tables were still set up from the night before, but the guests' faces looked like they were at a funeral.

'The guests who weren't staying in the hotel itself were staying in the lodges in the grounds,' Barrett volunteered. 'The group you're looking for are over there.' He nodded in a vague direction until Harry looked at him and he backed up the nod with a pointing finger.

'Well, that narrows it down a bit,' Harry said.

'The young woman with the green polo shirt sitting next to the man...'

'Got it.' He walked over with Dunbar and Alex.

'Where's your cohort, Jimmy?' Harry asked, almost saying *sir* again. He knew he would be fucked if he let that slip out even once.

'He's going to get his arse kicked when I get a hold of him. He was here a minute ago. Probably got one of the bridesmaids upstairs for a private interrogation. That laddie has a one-track mind that's going to get him in trouble one day.'

'Let's just err on the side of caution and hope he's busy questioning some older guests.'

'I'll go and see what he's up to,' Dunbar said. 'You can come with me and get me up to speed,' he said to Barrett. 'We'll see if anybody remembers seeing anything.' They walked away.

Harry and Alex pulled out a chair without any arguments from the three people at the table.

Harry made the introductions.

'I'm Claire Blythe, Marie's best friend and chief bridesmaid,' the young woman said, her lip trembling briefly before she regained her composure.

'Laurence Spencer, Duncan's best man. Call me Larry.'

'We need to ask you a few questions, which might seem awkward at first, and you might wonder why we're asking, but when somebody goes missing, we have to establish some sort of background,' Harry said. 'Most times, people get hacked off and leave without saying a word, and then come back, though a fair number of people don't come back. But it's very unusual for a bride to go missing on her wedding night.'

Claire looked at him. 'You might want to find that bastard Dubois, then,' Claire spat, spittle flying.

'We were told about her ex-fiancé,' Alex said. 'We'll have somebody go and look for him in Edinburgh.'

'They won't find him,' she answered.

'Why not?'

'Because he's not in Edinburgh, he's here.'

'You saw him?' Larry said.

'Yes. I didn't see him at the cathedral because of all the excitement, and I only caught a glimpse of him last night, because he was in here.'

'Why didn't you tell the police?'

'What do you think I'm doing?'

'Are you two a couple?' Alex asked.

'What? No,' Larry answered, making a face.

'You don't have to look like that. You would do well to be going out with me.'

Larry made another face as Claire turned away.

'Did Dubois say anything to you?' Harry asked.

'No. I just saw him walking about, all dressed up as

if he was part of the wedding party. Nobody questioned him. They were all too busy getting drunk and doing the conga.'

'Have you seen him today at all?'

Claire shook her head. 'No. It was a hectic night. We started off looking for Marie, but then they called the police. They came but there wasn't much they could do. I think they thought there had been an argument and Marie was hiding somewhere. I didn't see him again.'

'Can I ask how well you know Marie?' Alex said.

'We met at college. Glasgow School of Art.' She looked at the two detectives. 'I know, right? Art college. She could have gone anywhere, but her dad's a millionaire and she wanted to do something fun, so she studied design, like me. We ended up renting a flat together for our time at college and she was so much fun. Not like some other stuck-up tossers who don't want to get their hands dirty.'

She threw a quick glance at Larry.

'What about boyfriends?' Harry said. 'Before Dubois came on the scene?'

'She didn't have many. I mean, yes, we went out drinking and had a few laughs, but she didn't sleep around. Despite what other people thought. But we had a few good times and she went out with a couple of guys, nothing serious, until she met Vince.'

'Who broke it off?' Alex said.

'She did. Vince was gutted. I've never seen a grown man cry so much.'

'He saw the money flying out the window, no doubt,' Larry said.

'What?' Claire said, rounding on him. 'Do you think everybody who goes out with somebody who has a bit of money is only after the cash?'

'There *is* a certain attraction to it,' Harry said. 'I've seen it many times.'

Claire looked at him. 'I don't think Vince was like that. I mean, he wasn't in the same league financially, but he ended up with a good job at a computer games company as a designer. And Marie obviously wasn't bothered by it.'

'Did she ever say why she spilt up with him?'

Claire looked down at her hands before looking back up and locking eyes with Harry. 'They had a fight over something. She never did say what, but I overheard her one night, on the phone with Vince.'

'What did she say?'

'I couldn't make out the words, just the sound of arguing.'

'We'll see if anybody saw him.' Harry looked at Larry. 'How about you, Mr Spencer? When did you last see Marie?'

'I already gave a statement.'

'I know. And this is why we ask again; in case you remember something else that you didn't at the earlier interview.'

'Do I need a lawyer?'

You might need a plastic surgeon if Broderick Gallagher finds out it was you who had something to do with his daughter going missing, Harry thought. 'You've been watching too many re-runs of *The Bill*. We're asking you to talk to us so we can see if there's any way we can locate your friend's new wife. If you don't want to help us, you can walk away. But then you'll automatically be the number one suspect.'

'Good golly. I was with Duncan the whole time. He can testify to that.'

'Run me through the events leading up to you last seeing Marie.'

Larry took a deep breath and let it out slowly, whether giving himself time to fabricate some lies or whether to blow out the mental cobwebs, Harry wasn't sure.

'The DJ announced that the happy couple would be going upstairs to get changed. Duncan wanted me to accompany him as he had a gift for me. Marie wanted *her,*' nodding to Claire, 'to help her unzip the dress. So the four of us went upstairs. The women went into Marie's room and Duncan and I went into his. We had a drink, he gave me the engraved tankard, and he went into the en suite to get changed. When he came out, we went into the hallway and Claire was there, waiting for us.'

'How long did it take for Duncan to get changed?'

Larry shrugged. 'Fifteen, twenty minutes. We had a couple of nips and reminisced about our past. Had a laugh.'

'Does that timeline seem right to you?' Alex asked Claire.

'Yes. It took a little bit of fiddling to get Marie's dress zip down. But I helped her fold it and get it into the box. Then we had a glass of champagne. I left her and she said she would be down in a minute. I waited in the hall and a few minutes later those two came out. The three of us headed downstairs to wait and later on somebody alerted us that Marie was gone.'

One of Larry's friends came over. 'They're going to feed us now. They've been preparing a buffet and they're going to bring food out. The search is being called off and the staff and other volunteers are coming in. Too dangerous in the pitch dark.'

'Thanks, Raffles.' Larry stood up next to his friend. 'I hope I helped. But if you ask me, I think Marie saw her ex, they got chatting and she's fucked off with him. And Duncan will hit the roof if that happened.'

'Well, thanks for that input,' Harry said. *Don't give up your day job, inspector.*

Dunbar came into the room as Larry walked away. 'They're calling it off for the night.'

'I know. Inspector Morse there just told us.' Harry stood up and stretched. 'They're putting food out for us all. Well, I'm assuming we're included.'

'Fucking right we are. I'm not spending my weekend off up here without getting a free scran.'

'Too right. Come on, Alex, we can get a bite then decide what's happening tomorrow.'

'How many of the original guests are still here?' Alex asked.

'Around fifty,' Dunbar answered. 'They're staying one more night then they're off. Nothing to keep them here except for helping us with our enquiries. The rest had to leave to go back to work tomorrow.'

'Right.'

'How many stewards work here?' Harry asked. 'The guys who are dressed in all the kilts and regalia.'

'There are twenty-five of them. Including the head steward, Angus McPhee. They're all still out searching.'

They were walking towards the ballroom where the food was being laid out. 'Let me ask you this, Jimmy. How do we know Marie didn't just leave in a car with her ex?'

Dunbar stopped. 'Truth is, we don't.'

SIX

Harry had showered and changed into some casual clothes. They had moved into their respective rooms upstairs, with Broderick Gallagher blustering about how people should be out looking for his little girl. Harry was impressed with his room and soon found the mini bar.

'In case of emergencies?' Alex said.

'This is an emergency, sergeant; I'm up here in the Highlands of Scotland and my bottle of Scotch is back home.'

'Slàinte,' she answered, holding her glass up for Harry to clink.

'I don't know what I'm more impressed with, you using big words or drinking whisky.' He clinked her glass.

'I'm a lady of many talents.'

'Just don't say that in front of Jeni Bridge.'

At which point Jeni answered the FaceTime call on Harry's iPad.

'Good evening, commander,' Harry said.

'How are things there, McNeil?' Jeni cut to the chase.

'DS Maxwell and I are just going over things now, and to be honest, there are no signs of foul play and nothing to suggest she didn't just up and leave.'

Jeni's face looked surreal on the smaller screen. 'We're forgetting one thing. It was her wedding night. You're married, aren't you McNeil?'

'Was, ma'am.'

'Well, I'll bet your ex was in love with you on your wedding night. I can't imagine why any woman would leave her new husband.'

'Marie Gallagher's ex-fiancé is here, too,' Alex said. 'A witness spotted him sneaking around on the wedding day but we don't know where he is now.'

'Any chance she left with him?'

'That's something we're considering,' Harry said.

'Are they still looking for her?'

'It's dark now,' Alex said. 'They're calling it off and getting everybody back inside. The property has twenty thousand acres and it's pitch black out there. It's getting dangerous.'

'What about her mobile?'

49

'There's no sign of it,' Harry said. 'It's not switched on so it's not pinging. Her wedding dress is also missing. Her purse and handbag and all her other belongings that she brought up here with her are still in her room.'

'How many guests are still there?'

'Most of them. About fifty or so. A lot of them left after being questioned, as technically this isn't a crime scene. A lot of them have to go to work tomorrow, but the family are here. Some friends.'

'I've been in touch with the chief constable and he's authorised any overtime and expenses. Apparently, he golfs with the good Mr Gallagher. He's keen to be seen to be helping out by supplying officers to help in the search.'

The chief was Jeni Bridge's ex-husband. Harry got the feeling Jeni didn't take any crap off him.

'How long are you wanting us to stay up here?' Harry asked.

'We'll give it another couple of days. Call me every day for an update. We'll go from there.'

'Will do.'

'I'll talk with you tomorrow night.'

Jeni hung up, not knowing she would be talking to Harry a lot sooner than that.

He finished his whisky. Alex sat holding her glass, Harry looking at her.

'Oh. You want me to leave, don't you?' she said.

'Not at all. But if I FaceTime Vanessa and she sees you in my room, she'll make our deaths look like an accident.'

She finished the whisky and stood up. 'As parties go, this one will go down in the annals of history as being the least exciting one I've ever been to.'

'At least you didn't have to pish in a bucket.'

'It was close though.' She grinned and left the room.

Harry sent a FaceTime call to his girlfriend. No answer. He would try later. If he remembered. Vanessa wasn't the only one who could play games.

SEVEN

'In the name of fuck, what are we doing out here?' Tom Gunn said. 'You know what I think? I think she got married to him, shat herself because she knew she had made a mistake, then fucked off without him.'

'Shut up, you moron,' Sharon Gallagher said. 'That's my bloody sister you're talking about.'

'That's what *you* told me! That she had doubts.'

'Okay, now you need to rein it in. Somebody will hear you.'

'At this point, I couldn't care less. I mean, look at us; it's pitch black, it's starting to piss down, we can't see anything beyond the light from the torches and I'm knackered. This has been a shite wedding. Next time I get an invite to one of your dad's dos, I'm going to tell him to shove it up his jacksy.'

'Christ, you do nothing but moan.' She looked up at the canopy of trees, as the rain fell harder. 'And I'm sure my father would appreciate hearing you talk like that. Give him time to arrange somebody to slap you.'

'I've got plenty to moan about though, haven't I?'

'We're going home tomorrow. Just make the most of it.'

Tom suddenly smiled. 'I'm going to make the most of it tonight when we get back to the room.'

'Like I'm going to be in the mood.'

'Fuck's sake,' Tom said under his breath. 'Another reason to not piss on Gallagher should he ever find himself on fire.'

They were on some sort of old track. The steward who was in charge of their pitiful search party said there wasn't much chance of Marie being out here, but they had to check.

'She'll get a piece of my fucking mind if we catch her lording it back in Edinburgh,' Tom said. 'Did you hear that somebody saw her ex, that arsehole, Vince Dubois?'

'What? Vince, here?' Sharon said. 'I don't believe it.'

'Believe it, sister. I think she caught sight of him and would have jilted dogface at the alter if she'd seen Vince earlier, but she didn't see him until it was too late, then thought she had married the wrong man. Now Vince will be giving it laldy with her in a nice warm hotel room somewhere while us twats are out in the fucking woods—'

'Hey! Tommy Gunn!' one of the party further up ahead shouted. Eddie Lister, Tom's friend.

'I told that arse that not to call me that. It's fucking Tom, not Tommy,' he said to Sharon. 'What's he bleating about now anyway? Probably got a splinter or something.'

'Tommy!' the man shouted again. Not counting the steward, there were five of them, and Tom's friend was the only other man in the group.

'Are you coming up here or what?' the friend shouted.

'I'm coming!' Tom shouted back. *Fucking nob end.* He strode up the incline. The rain was coming down hard now, and the track was getting wider as it opened up into a clearing.

'What is it?' Tom said, but he was looking at what his friend's torch was highlighting; an old lodge. 'What the fuck is that place?'

'That steward bloke told us there are old lodges scattered about here. This is obviously one of them.'

'She wouldn't be in there,' Tom said, his lip turning up in disgust. 'And even if she is, she's fucked. I'm not going in there. What if one of us fell and broke a leg?

You know how far back it is to the Land Rover? I'm not carrying any of the women. Not even Sharon. I mean, she's not huge, but I have a dicky leg.'

'Let's hope your leg doesn't give out when you you're back in the room then.'

'Look, it's some shitey old building that's probably infested with rats. There's no way she's in there.'

Lister had been shining his torch at the window on the ground floor. He switched it off.

'Fuck me,' Tom said, feeling the hairs on the back of his neck stand up. He was looking at a small light in the window.

'A candle?' Lister asked.

'Fucked if I know, but Soapy Soutar can go in there. He's in charge of this party. Where is he anyway?'

Tom shined his own light towards the back of the three women, who were huddled together now. Tom thought they might be comparing his and Lister's willie size but couldn't be sure. Then one of them giggled, and he hoped it wasn't Sharon.

'Where the fuck is he? Christ, he's supposed to be leading us.' He turned to Lister. 'Did you see him coming up here?'

'No. I thought he was keeping an eye on us from the back.'

'Lazy bastard is probably sitting in the Land Rover

eating some porridge or something.'

'He looks a bit of a hard bastard. I wouldn't say that to his face.'

'Fuck 'im. There's two of us. If he starts his pish, I'll stick the bastard.' Tom pulled out a little penknife and struggled with the blade for a second before springing it open.

'What are you going to do with that? Trim his ear hairs?'

'Listen, if I get in close, he'll have fucking tears in his eyes.'

'From laughing, ya daft bastard. Didn't you say these stewards are all ex-army?'

'Aye, but our one looks like Daphne Broon with a beard. A good kick up the kilt and he'll be walking like John Wayne just got off a horse.'

'He's not wearing a kilt. He's got waterproofs on like us.'

'Figure of speech.'

Lister put his torch back on and shone it back towards the women. The canopy of trees wasn't helping keep the rain off them much. They were holding their jackets above their heads, the ones that had been supplied by the hotel.

'Any of you seen Oor Wullie?' Tom shouted.

'Shut up, for fuck's sake,' Lister said, cringing. 'I don't want to get this battered and bruised.' He put the torchlight on his own face for a split second.

'Again, if push comes to shove, it's two against one. And besides, if he did manage to get the better of us, old man Gallagher would sort the bastard out. There would be a new tree planted out here with its own compost underneath.'

Lister shone the flashlight past the group of girls and found nothing but trees. 'It's a moot point now, because it looks like he's fucked off.'

'What?' Lister pointed his own torch in the same direction. 'Jesus.'

'I told you he was a weirdo.' He turned his torch back to the old abandoned lodge. 'Maybe he went by us and got into the house and lit a candle.'

'Why would he do that?'

'Who fucking knows. But somebody is in there.'

'We should go and have a look.'

'I told you, I'm not setting foot in there.'

'What if she *is* in there? Think of the brownie points you'll get with Sharon. Or better still, her dad.'

Tom thought about it for a moment. 'Come on then, ya smooth talking bastard.'

The lodge was a good five hundred yards into the woods, with the driveway covered in weeds and brush.

'I'm not taking the women in there. Just in case,' Lister said.

'Fine. We'll let them know to stay here and not split up. Safety in numbers and all that.'

'This is turning into a minging weekend.' Lister said.

'You're fucking minging. Shut up and go and tell the women we're going to have a wee deek at that old house.'

Lister walked away, mumbling to himself. He reached the women who protested a bit but he assured them they would only be a few minutes, before returning to Tom.

'If you're serious about settling down with Sharon, you should know she's a fucking nag.'

'Never mind that. You told them to stay?'

'I did but they're not happy.'

'Come on then, let's make this quick. If it seems okay, we can get them to join us and we can shelter from the rain. And when we see that bearded twat, we can tear a strip off him. And since Broderick owns the hotel, we can make sure the bastard gets fired.'

They walked through the long grass covering the drive until they got to the house. There were weeds and overgrown bushes everywhere. The lodge was built in the same way as might be found in the old wild west. It was made of logs, two storeys high, with a redundant chimney on the side. All around it was pitch black.

'This is the bit where the boy with the chainsaw jumps out and scares the shit out of us,' Lister said.

'Only in the movies,' Tom said, not quite believing his own words.

They walked up the steps to the front porch and saw the front door was ajar. The tiniest bit of light was leaking out. Lister turned back to see Tom climbing the steps behind him. He shone the torch back to the end of the driveway, but the women were sheltering under a tree and he couldn't see them.

Tom stood next to him. 'I swear to Christ, I'm going to boot that fucking jockstrap right in the nuts. Leaving us like this. We should make sure all of those caber tossers are fired.'

'Just stay focused. And stay alert.' Lister pushed the door and like in a horror film, it creaked when it opened. He flashed the torch around, the light dancing into every corner. It was a large, open-plan living room.

'Hello?' he shouted.

'Fuck's sake. You never seen a horror film? Why are you shouting? Letting the mad bastard know we're here.'

Lister turned to him. 'First of all, we don't know anybody's here.'

Tom turned to look at the candle sitting on the window sill. 'Who lit that, then, Santa Claus?'

Lister didn't have an answer. 'Just watch our backs.' He moved forward into the living room. A table was in the middle of the room, with two wooden chairs. Otherwise the room appeared to have been abandoned years ago.

The walls were made of board that had been nailed over the logs. The candlelight didn't do much to illuminate the room was enough to see something on the floor and the walls. Tom shone his torchlight on it.

'Jesus. Does that look like... blood, to you?'

Lister shone his own flashlight on it. 'Christ Almighty, it does.'

The two men looked at each other.

'Tell you what, if something happened in here, then it might be best if we tell them back at the hotel and we can come back when it's light.'

'Agreed. Let's get the fuck out of here.'

They didn't quite run, not until they hit the driveway, then it was every man for himself. Tom turned round once to see if there was a masked lunatic chasing them, but there was nobody.

He was out of breath by the time he reached the main track. Lister caught up. They stood for a few moments, calming themselves.

'Right, we tell the lassies that we checked the place

out but it looks dodgy, and we didn't want anybody getting hurt, so we'll come back when it's light,' Tom said.

'Got it.'

Suitably composed, they stepped further out into the track and shone the flashlight around.

The women were gone.

'Fuckin' magic,' Tom said. 'They can't do a simple thing like stay where they are.'

'I can't blame them. It's pissing down now, pitch dark and they don't want to be here just like us.'

'Well, fuck this for a game of soldiers. If they've gone back, then we're not going to be the pair of dafties who're hanging about.'

The rain eased off as they made their way down the track, their torchlight lighting the way.

'How long has it been now?' Lister said.

'About half an hour.'

'I thought we should have reached the Land Rover by now.'

'You and me both, Eddie, but you know what? I reckon that kilted freak went back and was sitting in the Land Rover and he saw the women coming, and fucked off with them.'

'The women wouldn't leave us behind. Would they?'

'Look around you,' Tom said. 'Do you see any sign of them?'

'I suppose not.'

Their boots crunched the stones on the drive as it levelled out a bit. 'The thought of sitting round a warm fire, drying off and drinking tea or waiting for us must have been a hard decision for them to make.'

'Maybe Sharon will be extra nice to you tonight.'

'Eddie, with each step I am getting more and more knackered. I'll be lucky if I can play a game of dominoes when I get up to the room.' He stopped so suddenly that Eddie bumped into him.

'What's wrong?' Lister said. 'You see the women?'

'I see something.' He looked at Lister. 'Burning. Look. Away in the distance, over there.'

'Christ, you're right. Do you think some bastard set the Land Rover on fire?'

'Maybe the women got a campfire going and now they're roasting marshmallows.' He looked at his friend and shook his head. 'How should I know? But there's one way we can find out.'

He started walking with renewed vigour. The track went beneath another canopy of trees and turned away to the right, towards the flames. They could see the flickering light a bit better through the trees now but their view was partially blocked by thick bushes on the side of the road. Then they rounded the bend.

'Jesus, Tommy, look at that!' Lister shouted.

They stopped and Tom looked. He couldn't quite make out the shape until they got closer.

'I don't believe it,' Tom said, then they both started running.

EIGHT

Harry McNeil was lying on his bed sleeping when he heard a banging on his bedroom door. He woke up and felt disoriented for a second, before remembering where he was.

More thumping on the door.

He got out of bed and grabbed a poker from the fireside set next to the unmade fire in the fireplace.

'Who is it?' he said without opening the door.

'Harry, it's me,' he heard Alex say from the hallway. He stood the poker against the wall behind the door before opening it.

'You have to come with me,' Alex said.

'Now, look. I'm old enough to be your... brother. You'll find somebody one day. Go back to your room.'

'Oh, you're very funny. But before you get ahead of

yourself there, Romeo, we have to go. They found Marie Gallagher.'

'I'm assuming it's not good news.'

'It's much worse than that.'

'Right, give me a minute to' – *dampen my hair down and brush my teeth* – 'get my shoes on.'

'Mind and wet your hair a bit. There's a tuft sticking up at the top. You weren't in bed already, were you?'

Harry ignored her and pushed the door closed and after quickly using the bathroom, he slipped his shoes and a jacket on. He'd fallen asleep fully dressed after trying to watch some Netflix.

'Right, tell me what's going on,' he said to Alex in the hallway.

'The shit's hit the fan big time. I'll tell you on the way. There's a car waiting for us downstairs.'

A Land Rover was outside with the engine running. Jimmy Dunbar and Sergeant Evans were already in the back of the big SUV, and it was obvious that Dunbar hadn't stopped to dampen down his hair.

'This is a right turn up for the books,' Dunbar said, before addressing the steward who was behind the wheel. 'Get going, son.'

The car headed down towards a road at the back of the hotel, in the direction of the new lodges, but then the driver took a left and they were on a dirt track.

'Somebody going to tell me what's going on?' Harry said.

'They found the lassie.'

'Murdered?'

'Oh, you could say that. She was put in a wheel-chair, left by the side of the road, and set on fire.'

'Jesus.'

'The Castle's fire brigade is up there now,' the driver said. 'We have our own fire engine and the main-tenance staff who live on site are the firefighters.'

The lights bounced through the darkness, illumi-nating trees, until they saw arc lights in the distance, sticking up from what Harry guessed was the fire engine. More Land Rovers were parked at the side of the road with the hotel's logo on their doors.

'Are we the first officers on the scene?' Harry asked Dunbar.

'Aye,' the driver answered. 'The Inverness crowd have been given a shout. They're staying down the road in a hotel. They've been alerted and the local plod are on their way, but you were given priority. It'll put some bastard's nose out of joint, mind.' He looked in the mirror at Alex. 'Excuse the French.'

'Edinburgh women swear, too, you know.' She shook her head and lowered her voice. 'Prick.'

Evans grinned.

The detectives got out of the car and were handed

torches by the driver, who also got out and stood at the front of the car, to get a better view of the now-deceased bride.

'Broderick Gallagher is going to go off his nut,' Dunbar said.

'Oh yes.' Harry saw something that looked vaguely human-shaped, sitting in what was left of a wheelchair, which was just the metal parts. He had to admit, the Castle fire brigade had done a good job at putting the fire out, but did wonder how they would cope if some-body torched the hotel.

He walked over to the firefighter with the white helmet, assuming he was in charge. 'DCI McNeil,' he said by way of introduction.

'Aye, I know who you are,' the man said. Then straight to business. 'We got a shout fifteen minutes ago, from two lads who were out with a search party. That's them over there.' He pointed to Tom Gunn and Eddie Lister.

'They came down with their search party?' Dunbar said.

The man turned to him, obviously displeased at having to turn to talk to another person before turning back and speaking to Harry.

'They came running down to the hotel. The others in the search party weren't with them. They were shouting in reception about a girl on fire. We got the call and they were driven back up to show us where they were talking about. When we arrived, the damage was done. Some of the grass was burning where petrol had spilled on to it, but it was extinguished. The body was smouldering, but no flames were visible. She was clearly dead.'

'You can tell it was a woman?'

'Those boys said they could see the bottom of a dress. It's burnt now, of course.'

Dunbar's phone rang and he took the call, stepping away from the others.

'What a way to go, eh?' Evans said. 'I mean, burning to death like that.'

The fire officer looked at him. 'She was already dead, before she was set on fire,' he said to the young DS.

'How do you know that?' Harry said.

The officer looked at him before answering. 'Because she has no head.'

NINE

Angus McPhee was standing near the firefighters, holding his radio. He spoke into it for a moment but Harry could only hear his voice, not make out the reply. The arc lights from the fire engine made the woods look like the set from a horror film.

Harry walked past him and approached the two young men, who were going to be the prime suspects for the time being. Jimmy Dunbar was at his side.

'Let's get them apart, Harry, and see what they've got to say for themselves.'

'They better hope they've got good memories if they've decided to come up with some fairy tale.'

Harry took Tom Gunn aside and introduced himself. 'Tell me what happened tonight.'

Tom took in a deep breath and let it out slowly.

'I'm fucking shaking, let me tell you.' He shook his head as if he was struggling to get his bearings.

Harry felt the chill wind come at them through the thick trees but concentrated on the man's face, looking for any signs of deception.

'We were in the search party. We started off in the recreation hall, an old building way behind the hotel. We split into groups. Him down there,' he nodded to McPhee, 'he gave us instructions. He went with another party and said he would come round and catch up with us, to make sure we didn't get lost. We were lumbered with some guy who has about as much personality as a sausage roll. He parked the Land Rover, we got out and started walking up the track. He said there were old lodges, but he didn't want to drive there as Marie might have walked towards them and fallen in a ditch or something.

'Then we got to an old driveway that led to a lodge. Me and Lister told the women to stay behind because Lister saw a candle in one of the windows. We thought Marie might be in there.'

'What's the name of the steward who was with you?'

'By the way he disappeared, Lord Lucan, I think.'

Harry looked at him.

'I don't know, alright? But I bet he doesn't get many women off Tinder knocking on his door.'

'Where was he when you saw the candle?'

'That's the thing. He was nowhere to be seen. The women were behind us, huddling together, but the guy was gone. I thought he'd legged it because he's lazy or something, but we went into the lodge, saw the candle, and not much else. When we came out and got to this track, the women were gone.'

'Did you look for them?'

'Well, we didn't don bush gear and run through the heather, if that's what you mean.'

'Don't be a smartarse, son. A woman's dead here, and you two were the ones to find her. You connect the dots.'

He looked aghast for a second. 'We didn't do it.'

'Tell me how you found her.'

'We couldn't find the women, so we thought they had just left, then when we walked down, the Land Rover was gone, so we thought the steward had maybe driven them down to the hotel since it was raining. We didn't hang around but started walking back. That's when we saw her in the wheelchair. On fire.'

Harry turned briefly, his eye catching the blackened corpse, before turning back to Tom.

'How do you know it was a woman?' He knew what the firefighter had told him, but he wanted to hear it from Tom's mouth.

71

'We could see a dress. It was like, above her knees but her top was on fire.'

'Did you stop to look closer?'

Tom looked disgusted. 'It was a corpse. She wasn't moving or making a noise. We didn't stop, we ran. Then when we got to the hotel, we told the receptionist.'

'Didn't you think of calling nine nine nine when you were up here?'

'Have you tried getting reception up here?'

Harry nodded. The signal was fine in the hotel, but out here in the middle of nowhere might be a challenge. 'Then what?'

'We were asked to show them where it was. The fire engine came up behind us and then they took care of it. Then that big guffy down there came in a Land Rover and started shouting. Well, we'll see how loud he fucking shouts when Broderick finds out.'

Harry looked back at Angus McPhee and saw the man having a heated conversation with their driver who had brought them up.

'Is that the man who drove you up there the first time?'

'No. That guy's bigger. Our driver was a wee short-arse.'

Jimmy Dunbar walked up to Harry and he stepped aside so they could compare notes.

'Sounds about right,' Dunbar said, 'unless they're pretty good at sticking to their concocted story. But he didn't smell of petrol. Did yours?'

Harry shook his head. 'Did Lister mention the candle in the lodge?'

Dunbar nodded. 'Sounds a bit farfetched to me. You fancy taking your sergeant and young Evans there with those two miscreants? Check it out? I'm sure that steward will be glad to get away from Shuggy McNasty.' He nodded to the steward who was getting a dressing down from his boss.

'Aye. Marie had to have been kept somewhere before she was set on fire. And it's a bit suspicious that the steward who drove them there disappeared and then they see the corpse on fire.'

'I want him found, Harry. He might have taken the women. And it's looking like he might have taken Marie.'

'I'll take them up there now.' Harry motioned for Alex. 'Go and tell Evans and our driver we're going for a wee jaunt in the woods.'

Alex looked at him. 'Any particular reason?'

'Those two witnesses are coming with us. He gave me some spiel about a candle in a window in an old lodge.'

'Right. But before we go, I'm going to have a uniform frisk them.'

'Good idea.'

While they were being frisked, Harry walked up to McPhee. 'The women who were in this group are unaccounted for. Have you been in touch with the driver who was with them earlier?'

'Andy?'

Harry glowered at him. 'I haven't personally been introduced to him, but if that's his name, then yes, I mean Andy.'

'I haven't been able to reach him on the radio.'

'What about the car he was driving?'

'It's missing.'

Harry thought about this for a moment. 'What sector were you in?'

'I was going between sectors, getting updates and making sure everybody was alright. I only heard about this from one of my men.'

'Tell me about this guy Andy. Like, what's his last name, for a kick-off.'

'Andy Buchan. Good guy. Bit quiet, but he was a hell of a soldier.'

'You guys know how to look after yourselves out here, don't you?'

'We do. We've trained for it. Especially since Mr Gallagher bought this estate. It never used to belong to the hotel, or the castle as it was years ago. But they bought two other estates, quadrupling the size of the place. There's big plans for here, with shooting lodges, and all sorts of things. It's a huge place but the tracks are going to be repaired, and the lodges are all going to be pulled down and rebuilt. It's going to be a massive estate when we're finished.'

'And I'm assuming this Buchan knows his way around?' Harry said.

'As we all do. It's our job to look after the guests. There are already new lodges built, and we not only look after the rooms, but we escort them on shooting trips into the hunting areas.'

Harry nodded, wishing he'd put on a heavier jacket. He'd forgotten how cold it got up in the Highlands.

They'd snagged a couple of uniforms too and had them ride with them in the Land Rover. If the two witnesses turned out to be psychos, then they'd be outnumbered and could be overpowered. In theory. Harry had seen the best laid plans go awry before.

'Tell the driver where to go, son,' he said to Tom. The two uniforms sat on the bench seats way in the back of the big car, with Lister sitting opposite. Tom was in the second row between Alex and Evans while Harry sat up front, hoping that Alex was on the ball should Tom Gunn decide to reveal himself as a nut job and wanted to kill them all.

'It doesn't seem that far when you're driving, but it

was a hoor of a trek down here. And it was pissing down at first. God knows why we allowed ourselves to be persuaded to come up here.'

'You know Andy Buchan well?' Harry asked the driver, as the four by four handled the track with ease, the headlights picking out nothing but trees and bushes.

'We all know each other, but Andy was one of the least talkative guys.'

'He hardly said a word to us,' Lister said from the back. 'I didn't want to start talking to him in case I couldn't get away.' He made a face. 'But listen, pal, if your mate's touched our girlfriends, he'll be getting his bollocks booted, no matter how many of you bastards there are. There are a lot more of us bastards down in Edinburgh.'

'Shut up,' Tom said, turning to his mate.

'Good idea, Mr Lister,' Harry said. 'Just concentrate on showing us where this lodge is.'

'There!' Tom shouted.

The headlights picked out the overgrown driveway and the driver turned left into it. The canopy of tall trees showered them with raindrops from the leaves as the wind shook the branches above.

'Stop,' Harry ordered.

The driver jumped on the brake like somebody had just run out in front of them.

'Kill your headlights.'

The man did and darkness came at them from all sides. There was no light to be seen anywhere. Harry turned to Gunn. 'Where's the candlelight?'

Tom moved forward in his seat and squinted. 'I can't see it now.'

'You're sure this is the place?'

'Yes. We didn't see any other driveways.'

Harry looked forward again. 'Drive on.'

The steward put the headlights back on continuing up the drive and stopping right in front of the old lodge.

Harry once again turned to the others. 'You two, come with us. The driver can stay here.'

They got out into the dark and took out their torches. The car was still running and lit up the front of the house.

The climbed the old rickety steps up to the porch and Harry looked at the two young men. 'If you're yanking my chain, you know what will happen, right?'

'We're not yanking your chain,' Tom said, his lip curling up, as if he was insulted the detective should even consider such a thing.

'I'm going in. I want you, Evans, right behind me, and Alex, you follow those two. Ready?' He nodded to the two uniforms at the back.

They all nodded. Harry opened the door and the

smell hit him. Not of decay, but the smell that some-body makes when their body has voided its contents.

'Jesus Christ, this is worse than before,' Lister said. 'It's boggin in here.'

Harry shone the torch around and they turned to the right and went into the living room. The beams cut through the gloom. He found a light switch but nothing happened when he flicked it. A staircase was in front of them.

'You two check upstairs,' Harry said and watched as the two sergeants went up to the next level.

'It looked like blood on the walls over there.' Tom stopped and pointed. Harry went over, shining his torch about.

'It could be blood,' he said, but then he looked at the spatter on the wall. Blood with little bits mixed in. *She doesn't have a head.* Harry knew where the burning corpse had been before she was put in a wheelchair.

He straightened up then looked round the corner. 'Jesus.' His voice was barely above a whisper for a moment before he turned to Alex and Evans.

'Cuff them both!'

The uniforms grabbed hold of Tom Gunn and Eddie Lister and handcuffed them.

'What's going on?' Tom said.

'Keep them there,' Harry said by way of an answer. 'Don't let them come round here.'

He walked closer to the chair by the small, square table and looked at the bloody corpse sitting on a chair. What was left of... him? He couldn't be sure. The head was gone, just like the woman in the wheelchair.

He ignored the two handcuffed men as he shone the light around the dining area. More blood on the walls. And what was left of the victim's head.

Rain started lashing down on the roof. He thought he heard a noise coming from upstairs, but it could have been the rain.

The light jabbed into the darkness, bouncing off the walls of the kitchen cabinets. There was nothing else here. He walked back to the corpse. It was dressed in wet weather gear just like the other people in the search parties were wearing.

He went through the pockets and found a wallet, opened it up and found a driving license: Andrew Buchan. The team leader of the search party who had come here. His radio was gone as well as his head.

He walked to the group of people in the hallway.

'Upstairs is clear,' Alex said.

'We have another victim. Let's get back to the car.'

'Who is it?' Alex asked.

'His ID says it's the steward who was driving this lot about.'

79

'He wasn't here a little while ago, I swear,' Lister said.

'Take them out to the car.'

They were taken out and Harry pulled up the hood on his weatherproof jacket.

He approached the driver's side of the Land Rover. 'Is there another way in to this lodge?'

The man nodded. 'Aye. There's always two roads that lead to them. The main one like this, and a service road into each one where we can stock up on supplies. I know because we've been told these are all going to be pulled down and they said the new ones will be exactly like the new ones over in the other sector. All these old lodges have a road running behind them so we won't get in the way of the guests.'

Harry nodded. 'Alex? With me.'

'What's up?' she said when Tom and Lister were safely in the back of the big car.

'We're just going to have a little look round the back. I want you to watch my back.'

'Not Evans?' she said. 'Or are you just being PC?'

'He's a clown. I want somebody I trust watching my back.'

Alex didn't know what to say for a moment. 'Lead the way.'

The rain was getting heavier by the minute. It fell

through the trees as if being thrown at them. Harry stopped and put a hand up.

'There's the garage there,' he said in a low voice. The grass and bushes were even more overgrown round here. The forest was slowly reclaiming the ground.

Alex took out her extendable baton and flexed it open.

Harry looked at it. 'You do realise that the two corpses had their heads blown off?'

'You got any better ideas?'

'Apart from going back and returning with armed response, no.' He walked forward and grabbed hold of the handle at the bottom of the garage door. He pulled up on it and it creaked and squeaked as he lifted.

He pointed for Alex to stand to one side and then got a hand underneath and gave it a shove. The door shot up and then silence. Nothing but the sound of the rain battering the branches and thunder exploding overhead.

Harry swung his flashlight around, then looked, ducking down and putting his head inside. He prayed the killer wasn't standing there with the gun.

He wasn't.

The lights picked out one of the hotel's Land Rovers sitting in the dark. Harry stepped forward and shone the light inside the vehicle. He cupped one hand against the glass but there was nothing inside.

'Empty,' he said. 'Let's get back to the hotel. Don't take your eyes off those two guys. This could be a game to them.'

They went back to the Land Rover and Harry told the driver to take them back.

Then suddenly, headlights lit up the back of the car. Harry and Evans got out as Angus McPhee walked up to them. 'Mr McNeil. You're wanted back at the hotel. There's been a development.'

TEN

Harry felt tired but the adrenaline was keeping him going.

'You look knackered,' Alex said to him as they got out of the big car.

'I feel it.'

'You need to get some rest.' She looked at him. 'When did Vanessa call it quits?'

He stopped, the rain pelting off his weatherproofs. 'What are you talking about?'

Alex shrugged. 'I'm just curious. I can see it's taking its toll. In the office this past week, you've looked knackered every day.'

'What makes you think Vanessa dumped me?'

'I'm a woman, Harry.'

Harry looked at her for a moment. 'A week ago.

She wants time to *get her head straight*. Quote unquote. I was going to FaceTime her, but she might think I'm begging. Now can we go inside?'

'We can indeed. I'm here if you want to talk.'

'About what?'

'Oh, you know, the price of cheese, stuff like that.'

They shook off the water as they made their way into the hotel entrance. People were rushing about like they were doing a fire drill but without the alarm sounding.

'Reminds me of the dark old days on the south side,' Dunbar said, shaking the water off his jacket. 'Pissing down, cold and full of nut jobs.'

They took their wet gear off in a side room before Harry found McPhee in reception. 'Have the family been told?'

McPhee turned to look at him. 'They were told to wait in the library, that there's been some news.'

'Right. I have some things to do then we'll be in to see them. Can you make sure they stay there?'

'Will do. I was just arranging for hot drinks to be taken in.'

Harry nodded and turned to Dunbar. 'We'll have to get the forensics crew up to the lodge after they've finished with the body.'

'Aye. They said they had finished photographing

the poor lassie before the rain came on, so they're going to head up there now. A couple of the stewards are going to take them, including our guy who drove us. Busy night for him, I think.'

'Sitting on his arse, driving a Land Rover about is hardly taxing his abilities,' Harry said.

'True. Lazy bastard.'

'Did you find out what the development is?'

The head of the forensics team came across to them. 'We're going up to that lodge. The Inverness team have been called back, but we were doing a search of the rooms again, and we discovered something. Duncan Randall's tux had blood on the front. We've taken it away for examination.'

'Where is Randall now?'

'I have no idea.'

'Thank you.' He described to her what the lodge was like and where the corpse was.

'Let's go and talk to the family, Jimmy.'

Dunbar took a deep breath and let it out. 'I wonder what they've got to say for themselves about the boy's suit having blood on it?'

'Just remember, money talks. Whatever it is, it will be swept under the carpet.'

'Or Randall will pull some strings for his son. They all walk on water in Glasgow.'

'And since Gallagher owns newspapers, he'll only allow his own people to talk to the guests, at least on the property. And they'll put a spin on it.'

In the library, Broderick Gallagher was a mess. Tears were running down his face and his eyes were red. Anne Gallagher was shedding some crocodile tears while she was bouncing her little boy on her knee. Harry wondered how well she got on with her step-daughter.

Gallagher looked up as the four detectives walked in. Both families were sitting in various chairs but each of them looked up as they entered.

'Is it my Marie?' Gallagher asked.

'We're not sure yet,' Dunbar said.

'How can you not be fucking sure? It's either her or it's not.' His face twisted with rage.

'It's not been possible to identify her,' Harry said.

Anne let a mask of fury rush over her face. 'What do you mean? We want to see her.'

'That won't be possible just yet.' *Not now, not ever.* 'She's been transported to Golspie hospital up the road before she gets taken for a formal post-mortem in Inverness.'

'But I'll still get to see my little girl, won't I?' Gallagher looked pleadingly at Harry.

'This is going to sound very clichéd, but you need

to remember the way she was. She isn't in a very good state.'

'What do you mean?' He stood up now.

'He means she was burnt, Mr Gallagher,' Dunbar said. Neither detective thought it prudent to tell him that there was no head on the corpse.

'Oh God, I can't believe it.'

'I have to ask,' Harry said, 'did she have any broken bones when she was younger?'

Gallagher looked into space for a moment. 'I... I can't think. Why?'

Anne looked up at him, her little boy looking confused. 'She has the pin in her arm above the elbow. Remember she fell off the horse when she was taking riding lessons a few years back and broke her arm?'

'Yes. Of course.' He looked at his wife before he looked back at Harry. 'You need that information to identify her?'

'Yes.' He watched as the Gallaghers sat back down. 'Did you know Marie's ex-fiancé was here?'

'What? Of course he isn't here.'

Claire was sitting behind them on a chair. 'He is here, Broderick. I saw him.'

Harry turned to Alex. 'Did you have the manager go through CCTV?'

'He said he would check. I left a photo of Dubois with a uniform.'

'Can you go and see if there are any results?'

She walked away.

'Where's Sharon?' Gallagher said. 'My other daughter. Somebody said they got separated from the two men they were with. One of them is Sharon's boyfriend.'

'The two men went into a lodge looking for Marie. When they came back out, the women were gone.'

'Gone? What do you mean, *gone*?'

'Right now, we're trying to locate them but this is a big area to search.'

'Where the bloody hell did they go? Call in as many people as you need. Money is no object.'

'We're doing everything we can. We'll have more volunteers tomorrow.' It was a lie, but Harry hoped the father wouldn't see through it. There was no way that any more volunteers were going out searching, not with a nutter on the loose, ready to shoot anybody.

'Sit down, love,' Anne said gently. The older man sat down and his son smiled at him.

Angus McPhee came in with a tray, followed by two female staff members. 'I thought you might like a cup of sweet tea,' he said, then left the room again.

'Tea. I want my bloody daughter, more like,' Gallagher said.

'The search has been called off for the night,' Dunbar said. 'It's getting too dangerous out there.'

Gallagher looked at him. 'Called off? Didn't you just hear me? I'll pay whatever it takes to have men out looking for my little girl!'

'Not while there's a possibility that somebody will pay with their life,' Harry said, and walked away.

ELEVEN

Monday morning started out with a coffee and toast for Harry. They were down in the dining room, a sense of foreboding lingering over the hotel like a plague.

Alex came in, poured some coffee and chose a cereal. Rain battered off the windows, giving them a not quite so warm Highlands welcome.

'Not got your sunglasses on this morning, I see,' Alex said, standing next to Harry as he sat at a table.

'That seat's taken,' Harry said, indicating the other three seats round the table.

'You lie. And don't think you can get rid of me that easily.' She put her cereal down.

'There's going to be a report written when we get back, and I have to tell you, it's not looking too good for you. I mean, you could redeem yourself by filling my coffee cup. Just saying.'

'Just so you know, I'm not running after you.'

'That's it, put a positive spin on it.'

She left and came back with a coffee and sat down.

'Next time, I'll go for them,' Harry said.

'Aye, you'd better. I'm marking it in my diary anyway, just to blackmail you with later.' She grinned and ate some cereal. 'Is this what you usually do? Get Vanessa to run after you, fetching coffee then she polishes your shoes for you?'

'She butters my toast for me between the coffee and shoe thing,' he said, sipping at his coffee.

'I've been up for ages. While you were pruning your eyebrows, I was down here. And guess what?'

'You didn't know how to spell muesli so you wrote down cornflakes on your breakfast order?'

'As much as you'd like that to be true, no. Broderick Gallagher sent his family home on his private jet this morning. They left a little while ago to drive down to Inverness.'

'Really? What about all that talk last night about how money was no object and he'd hire Robin Hood and his merry men to go traipsing through the woods looking for his daughter?'

'It was all piss-and-wind. His wife has gone back home with their little boy. Something about overseeing the business while Gallagher stays up here. Randall's family too, but they're not sharing a jet.

They each have their own. Randall himself is still here.'

'I was sitting in bed reading last night, when I started thinking.'

Harry gave her a look, about to make some disparaging remark, when Alex held up a hand. 'Just remember who's driving you home. But anyway, I got to thinking about Duncan Randall.'

'What about him?'

'Don't you think it's funny how we never see him? I mean, where is he now?'

Harry looked at his watch; eight thirty am. 'I'm sure he's grieving the loss of his wife.'

'He wasn't with the family last night. I checked. When they found out, he was nowhere to be seen. He still isn't.'

Harry looked up as Terry Randall walked in, looking ten years older than he did the day before. Harry stood up. 'Mr Randall. Can you spare us a minute?'

The older man walked over, looking more like a worn out car salesman than the king of the empire.

'What is it? Do you have any news?'

'Not as such, no, but I have a question. How long did Duncan know Marie before they decided to get engaged?'

'Why?'

'Just curious.'

'They met a couple of years ago. They got engaged after a year, and... well, you know the rest.'

'Okay. Where is Duncan now?'

'Up in his room, I suppose. Do you need to talk to him?'

'Yes. We'd like to ask him some background questions. Nothing to be worried about. We want to catch Marie's killer as soon as, and anything, any snippet of information can sometimes break a case.'

'When I see him, I'll tell him to come and find you.' He walked away.

'He's probably wondering what's going to happen to his little empire,' Jimmy Dunbar said, coming up to the table.

'You heard what he said?' Harry asked.

'I overheard because I was listening in. Nosy nebber, my wee lassie used to say.'

'Get some breakfast then grab a pew, sir,' Alex said.

'Don't mind if I do, sergeant.'

Dunbar walked over to the buffet table and took some toast and coffee before joining them. 'I had a hoor of a sleep last night, and now my old joints are creaking.' He looked at Harry. 'How about yours?'

'Never been fitter.'

'Delusional or liar, your choice,' Dunbar said to Alex.

'I'll toss a coin.'

'When you two are finished slagging me off, I'd like to get some plan of action going for today.'

'Relax, Harry. Time for coffee first.' He looked around. 'Where's that heid banger got to? I told Evans to be down here at eight thirty. He's done hee-haw since we got here. He's doin' my bloody tits in.'

Just then, DS Evans strolled in and smiled when he saw Alex.

'Good morning. I'm surprised to see you sitting with the old coffin dodgers.'

'Shut up. Grab a pot of coffee and bring it over here,' Dunbar said. Then, 'That laddie's doolally. If he spent more time thinking about this case than posting shite on Instagram, then maybe he'd get more work done.'

'I heard that,' Evans said.

'You were meant to. And don't get any of that bloody hair gel on the coffee pot.'

Evan sat down. 'Five hours sleep and I'm raring to go. *And* without the added benefits of medication.'

'Good for you,' Harry said. 'Just wait another twenty years and you'll have some young Jock pulling *your* pisser.'

'Better to die young. Go out in a blaze of glory.'

'Considering a young lassie was burnt to death, maybe keep that opinion to yourself,' Harry said.

'Anyway,' Dunbar said, pouring more coffee for everybody, 'they're going to start the search for those girls shortly. I spoke to Angus McPhee and he says his men want to go out searching, and suggested they take some of the hunting guns with them, but I told him there's more chance of Scotland winning the world cup than there is a bunch of gung-ho ex-soldiers going out there with guns. I mean, for God's sake. It's not grouse they're after.'

'Or ducks,' Harry said, looking at Alex. She pretended not to hear him.

'And now that a lot of the guests have gone home, we don't have that many suspects,' Evans said.

'Have a word with yourself,' Dunbar said. 'Do you think it's Marie Gallagher's granny who shot her? Or one of her old cronies? We can go through the wedding list and start narrowing it down.'

A man in a suit walked over to Harry. 'We were finally able to track down a timeframe on the CCTV with the man you were asking about in it.'

'I'll come and look.' He got up from the table and followed the man through a door behind the reception area and into an office.

The view on the TV screen was paused. The man played it, rewound it a little then hit play again.

Vince Dubois was clearly seen walking out of the hotel and into one of the hotel's Land Rovers.

'Can you see who's driving it?'

The man shook his head. 'It's impossible to tell, but we see the time stamp, so I can ask McPhee who would be driving around that time, see if he knows.'

'Okay, thanks. Let me know when you get something.'

Harry left the office and saw McPhee going into the dining room. He called him over.

'I'd like you to take a look at a CCTV picture and see if you can hazard a guess as to who is behind the wheel of one of your Land Rovers by the time stamp.'

'Sure.' They walked back into the office and McPhee had a look. 'That's me driving.'

Harry looked at him for a moment. 'You drove him?'

'Yes. Was there a problem?'

'Where did you take him?'

'We were at the stables, breaking into groups. He asked me where he could go and join the others to help search for Marie. I told him I was going there and I would take him. I dropped him off when I got to the stables and there were quite a few people hovering about.'

'Did you see him after that?'

'I can't tell, to be honest. I was focused on getting my men into groups with the guests. He was just another face.'

Harry nodded. 'Thank you.'

Just then, his radio crackled as Harry started walking away, then McPhee put a hand on his arm. 'That was a call coming through on the radio. It's rough, but Sharon Gallagher is one of the lassies that's missing, yes?'

'Yes. What about her? Has somebody found her?'

'I'm not sure. I just heard the name and the words *Clover House*.'

'What does that mean?'

'All the old hunting lodges were given names of flowers by the previous owner. I know that because we have them marked on the maps so we know where we're going and what we're searching.'

'Get some four by fours round the front. I'll get my team. You know where this place is, right?'

'Aye.'

'Then move, man!'

Harry ran back into the dining room and Alex was up in a flash. 'What's happening, sir?'

'McPhee just got a call on the radio. Somebody told him where Sharon can be found.'

'Where abouts?' Jimmy Dunbar said as he and Evans stood up.

'One of the old lodges. He's getting some cars round the front so we can go and look.'

'Let's go. Move it, Boaby!' Dunbar shouted when Evans stopped for a quick chug of his coffee.

Randall rushed over. 'What's happening?'

'Go and get Gallagher and wait in the library for us,' Dunbar said and they left the room.

TWELVE

The big Land Rover bumped its way down a rough road, followed by two others. The lead car had four armed response officers and the detectives were wearing stab-proof vests. 'I don't think this will stop a shotgun, somehow,' Dunbar said. 'We can always shove young Boaby in front of us though, use him as a shield.'

'You're not funny, sir,' Evans said. He had a worried look on his face.

Harry smiled, but he felt the adrenaline rushing through him.

Crackling came through on the radio, and the Land Rover stopped. The lead car was being driven by a police officer and it turned right into an overgrown driveway.

The house had to be checked by the armed officers before they could go in. Harry looked through the windows of the Land Rover behind them and saw the ambulance holding back at a distance.

'I hope to Christ she's alive,' Harry said, 'but if we're going by what's already happened, it's not looking good.'

'Who called over the radio?' Alex asked.

'Nobody knows. They're thinking the killer took Andrew Buchan's radio and he's now using it.'

Alex looked puzzled and mouthed *Buchan?*

'The driver who took Tom Gunn and the women up to the lodge. The one who we found dead last night.'

They sat and waited, the diesel engine droning away the only sound in the car. Everybody sat waiting for a radio to kick in, or the sound of gunfire to erupt through the woods.

Nothing happened.

A few minutes later, an officer with a machine gun approached their Land Rover.

'There are two young women in there. They're being brought out now, sir.'

Harry nodded then they all filed out and walked up to the lodge, which was in worse shape than the one they'd been in the previous night.

The ambulance crew made it past the parked cars and escorted the women out of the house and into the back of the ambulance.

'Where's Sharon?' Harry asked.

They were both sobbing and it took a moment for them to calm down.

'She's gone,' one of them said. 'He took her.'

'Who did?'

The women stopped crying for a moment. 'We didn't see his face. He was dressed in waterproofs, just like everybody else, but he had a mask and a hood on. He brought us here and tied us up, then he took Sharon.'

'How long ago did he take her?'

'Last night, right after we were taken at gun point. I'm not sure of the time.' The woman started crying again.

'Thank you. You're going to be taken to the hospital for a check-over then I'll have somebody take a statement.'

He walked away and spoke to Dunbar. 'He took Sharon.'

'I think those two laddies that took us to the other lodge are in deeper than they're saying.'

'Could be. It fits in with the timeline. Have them taken to the station for more questioning.'

Dunbar turned to Evans. 'You heard the man. Get on it. You might get a Boy Scout badge if you get this right.'

Evans nodded. 'Sir.'

'I'd like us to get back and have a talk with Angus McPhee, see if he has any idea where the killer could have taken Sharon,' Harry said.

'There's not much else we can do until forensics goes over the place,' Dunbar agreed as they returned to the Land Rover to head back to the hotel.

'Broderick Gallagher is already on the edge,' Harry said, 'and this is just going to be the shove that puts him over.'

'You can have the pleasure of dealing with him. I have enough on my plate with Randall.'

'Talking of which,' Alex said, 'where's Duncan Randall?'

Nobody had any idea.

Terry Randall was standing in the reception area having a full-blown argument with Broderick Gallagher.

'I told my son not to marry that fuckin hoor!' he said, then deftly side-stepped the swing that came towards his face.

'Whoa, whoa,' Harry said, as Angus McPhee approached the two men. 'What's going on here?'

'This fuckin loudmouth, bleating on about his boy. Arsehole. I wish my Marie had never clapped eyes on that dim-witted fuck of a son.'

'Now we'll never have to see each other ever again,' Randall said. He was looking round McPhee.

'Don't worry, son, I won't sully my fucking hands on him.'

'Where's your son?' Dunbar said.

'I don't know. Out with a search party, probably.'

Dunbar looked at Harry before answering the man. 'There are no search parties out. Are you sure he isn't in the hotel?'

'I don't know where the hell he is. My wife has gone home. Like Gallagher's has. We didn't want them to be here while their lives could be in danger. I'll go and have a look around, see if I can find him.'

Harry took Broderick Gallagher aside. 'Look, sir, I'm sorry to have to tell you this. We got the women back—'

'Thank God!'

Harry held up a hand. 'I'm sorry to say, he took Sharon. We only found the other two.'

'What? For fuck's sake! Why is he doing this to me?'

'We need to find out why you're being targeted. Now, do you have anybody here that can be with you?'

Gallagher shook his head. 'They all went back to Edinburgh.'

'What about Marie's friend, Claire?'

'She's been a rock. But she went back home. She's one of the best designers on the team at my newspaper, not to mention my Marie's best friend.'

'Did she go home on the jet?'

'Yes. She went with Anne.'

Harry's phone rang. He listened to the caller before hanging up.

'The doctor wants me to go along to Golspie, to the hospital.'

'What's wrong?' Alex asked.

'They just want to talk to me about something.' He turned his attention to Dunbar. 'How do you want to play this? We have another woman missing and we know for a fact that there's a nutter loose with a shotgun. I don't want to put any civilians at risk.'

'Agreed. But the problem we have is, this place is so fucking big. What with all of those lodges scattered around, he could have taken her anywhere.'

'If you want my opinion,' Alex said, 'he's not going to shoot anybody other than his target, unless he maybe gets cornered. But he's on a mission.'

'And what would that be?' Dunbar asked.

'He's trying to get back at Broderick Gallagher. Now, our main suspect is Vince Dubois, who we know for a fact, was here. He has means, motive and opportunity.'

Harry waved McPhee over. 'Where would somebody get a hold of a shotgun?'

'We have an armoury. Where we keep the guns for the guests who haven't brought their own.'

'Which is where?'

'Down in the basement.'

'How many people have access to it?'

'All of the stewards. We receive the requests for the shotguns and we go down to the armourer – who is a trained firearms expert – and the guns are logged out.'

'Do you know if any are missing?' Alex asked.

'I can send a text and find out. But if one of our shotguns is being used, then it could be missing from one of the guests who logged it out.'

Harry gritted his teeth for a moment. 'Look, son, you already told us that this hotel has been closed for normal bookings this whole weekend because of the wedding, so you must have a rough idea of how many guests logged out a shotgun.'

'My apologies for the confusions, sir. I should have said that there are several families who are up here for a week. They wanted to stay after the wedding and do some clay pigeon shooting. The guns have already been logged out and were transported to the lodges and locked away in the gun cabinet that is in each lodge. I'll get a list of those who requested a gun.'

'Thank you.'

McPhee walked away.

'I have to call my team in Edinburgh, then we'll get over to the hospital,' Harry said.

'Do that,' Dunbar said. 'We'll hold the fort here.'

Harry left the hotel with Alex. 'I'm going to requisition a patrol car to take us to Golspie.'

'Betty will be most upset.'

'I couldn't care less if Thomas the Tank Engine is upset, we're going in a patrol car.'

'Fine, but you're sitting in the back of Betty on the way home.'

'You know they're going to think you're special if you keep on talking like this?'

'That's fine because I used to be a Special Constable.'

'And now you're a Special Detective,' he said in a slow voice.

Alex made a face as they got in the car.

THIRTEEN

They got a uniform to drive them to Golspie, which took no time at all. From the A9, the small hospital looked like a mansion house, but as they got closer, they could see the addition on the left-hand side with the Accident and Emergency sign above the door.

'Wait here for us,' Harry instructed as the driver pulled up to the main entrance past the A&E.

They walked up the steps to the front door and inside saw a woman sitting at a reception desk. 'We're looking for the mortuary,' Harry said, showing his warrant card.

She pointed them to the lift and told them it was one level down.

'I thought this place would be a lot smaller,' Alex said, as the lift doors closed.

'It's small enough. At least you won't get lost in here, unlike the old Royal Infirmary in Edinburgh.'

'That place used to give me the creeps. My granddad died in there.'

'And now it's flats. I wonder if your grandfather moved on or if he's still wandering about.'

'That's not very nice, is it? All the happy memories I have of him, then seeing him lying there in that bed. You've ruined them all.'

'If it's any consolation, my own grandfather died in the Western.'

'It's not. And didn't you say you were going to call the team back in Edinburgh?'

'I'll call DI Shiels after this.'

'You forgot. See? I am an asset to this team,' Alex said as the doors slid open.

'That's one way of describing it,' he said, as they walked along a brightly lit corridor, towards a sign that told them they were indeed going in the right direction.

Through a set of rubber doors, they were into the mortuary itself. A small office was over on one side. Two plate glass windows looked out into the main area. A woman was sitting at a desk, staring down at paperwork.

Harry knocked on the door.

'Fuck me,' the woman said, jumping back in her chair.

'DI Harry McNeil, DS Maxwell. I'm assuming that's Gaelic for *Welcome?*'

'No, it means, *Fuck me, you nearly gave me a heart attack.*'

Harry looked at the woman, who might have been in her early thirties. She was slim with dark hair and eyebrows that looked like they had been drawn on with a magic marker. The white coat she was wearing billowed out as she stood up. He thought she could have been a Goth in her early years, with the right hairdo and black lipstick.

'You get many patients coming back to life, then?' he said with a quiet smile.

'That would have been a first. Angie Patterson.' She held out her hand for him to shake.

He gently gripped it but he could feel a strength in her hand that her looks belied.

She let go and nodded to Alex.

'You'll be here to look at the burn victim,' Angie said, matter-of-factly.

'We are.'

'This way.' She turned right out of the office and Harry couldn't help himself; he looked down to see if she was wearing Doc Martens. She wasn't. She stopped at a row of fridges. She looked at the names for a second, as if they were all full and she couldn't remember where the body she was looking for was stored.

'Ah, here she is.' She turned to look at the two detectives. 'They're coming for her later today to do the PM in Raigmore.'

'I understand that. We just want a look.'

Angie gripped the handle and pulled out the drawer. 'I put her at waist level so it would be easy to look at her. The other headless body is in the next drawer. You want to see him too?'

'No, we know who he is.'

'There's only two more and they're further down. Poor old sods whose time on earth was over. But they've nothing to do with your case.'

'Why so many drawers here?' Alex said, counting fifteen.

'It goes back to the war. Bodies were housed here, but I think they expected there to be a lot more. There weren't that many, so I'm led to believe. My predecessor was a history buff.'

'What's your official title?' Harry asked.

'Mortuary attendant. Although I help out in records when we're quiet down here. Which is not that often, because we have the geriatric ward.'

Harry steeled himself to look at what was left of the young female. He'd been to many fatalities, but it was always the burn victims that got to him.

Marie looked exactly like she had last been seen in the wheelchair. She was lying curled on her side, having been fused by the fire. She had no head and most of her body was burnt. Except the bottom of her legs. A little piece of dress material clung onto the charred skin.

'I was told there was a pin in one arm,' Angie said, 'but I can't see anything like that. Then again, I didn't go to medical school, and they don't pay me the big bucks. But there's no pins in either arm. It would show, the way her skin is.'

'It was a long shot, but I thought maybe somebody could tell. And that was why I was asked to come along here.'

'Hang fire there. Are you always in such a hurry with a lady?' She looked at him with raised eyebrows.

'Only if I have a bus to catch.'

'Because his car is getting fixed,' Alex added.

Harry gave her his best *We'll talk about this in the car* look.

Angie looked at him. 'Look at this.'

He looked at the corpse but instead, she had pulled up her trouser leg. 'See it?'

'You didn't shave your legs in the shower this morning?' Harry said. Alex rolled her eyes.

'Other side,' she said.

'Oh. Nice.' *I suppose.* He was looking at a small

tattoo of a Scottish thistle behind a heart that had been filled with the Scottish Saltire.

Angie put her trouser leg back down. 'My point is, sometimes a woman will have a discreet tat. Not all women, but some, like me. It's not obvious at first.'

Please God, don't let her show me any piercings. 'And?'

Angie went around to the other side of the drawer and moved the headless corpse onto her other side. 'The legs didn't burn all the way down. They were covered in soot, but the bottom of the legs and feet weren't burnt. And you did say that your victim had no tattoos.'

Harry looked at her for a moment. 'Hold that thought.' He walked away back through to the small office and made a call to the hotel. Jimmy Dunbar promised to get right back to him. He sat on the edge of the desk while he waited. The small room had an old smell about it, like his granny's house. Like old furniture. Or his old primary school.

He could hear the two women chatting around the corner. As far as he was aware, Alex didn't have any tattoos, or at least, none that were visible. He didn't want to ask.

There was a calendar on the wall showing classic motorbikes. He wondered if Angie was a biker chick, or whatever else they were called. *Biker hoor* didn't have the same ring to it, and he thought she might kick his head in if he asked if that was what they were known as.

His phone rang, drawing his attention away from a Triumph. 'Hello?'

'I asked old man Gallagher. He about blew his fucking stack, Harry. He said Sharon has a tattoo like that. Why do you ask?'

'Because the woman we found burning last night isn't Marie – it must be Sharon.'

FOURTEEN

'Look at you, acting all innocent,' Alex said as the patrol officer dropped them off back at the hotel.

'The Highland air has obviously gone to your head.'

'Young Miss Angie has her sights on old Uncle Harry.'

'Were you dropped on your head when you were a baby or something?'

'Oh, come on, Harry. She gave you her number. *And* she showed you her unshaved leg.'

'No, she gave me the hospital's number and said I should call if I needed any more information. Weren't you listening? You *were* in the room.'

'Secret messages. There was an edge to her voice that would sound like purring if she were a cat.'

'I'm not listening to you anymore.'

They walked into the reception area to find chaos ruling.

'Jesus,' Jimmy Dunbar said, coming over to them, 'Gallagher's running about alternating between wanting to murder his daughter's killer with his bare hands, hiring a team of hit men and, burning the hotel down with, and I quote, *all of you useless bastards in it.*'

'He's upset, then?'

'Rightly so, but he's off the fucking scale, Harry.'

'I can understand why. Somebody made us believe that Marie was murdered, but it was his other daughter. I think it would drive me mad, too.'

'Let's get into the library where we can gather our thoughts.' Dunbar clapped a hand on Harry's shoulder and they moved away.

There were some of the junior detectives from Inverness in the library, along with Robbie Evans.

'We're going through CCTV right now, or at least we have some of the Highland Coo brigade doing it,' Evans said. 'We want to see if Marie can be spotted anywhere. And how in God's name is that her sister Sharon?'

Harry poured himself a quick coffee. 'I'm thinking, Marie was taken, or killed. Then he was watching the search party with Sharon in it. Then he took the steward and the women, killed the steward, and took Sharon away with him. He dressed her in Marie's dress, then killed her. He wanted us to think Marie was dead.'

'Why?' Alex said.

'To put us off the trail, as it were,' Dunbar answered.

'We don't know the *why* yet,' Harry answered. 'Why wouldn't he kill Marie? Unless Sharon was the real target.'

'You!' a voice shouted from the doorway. Broderick Gallagher. He was standing looking at Harry.

'Mr Gallagher, I'm sorry for your loss.'

'Fuck you. What the hell is going on?'

Harry walked over to him. 'It seems that somebody took Marie, then took Sharon and dressed her in Marie's clothes to put us off the scent.'

'Not to mention blowing her head off! You forgot that little nugget!' He was starting to shout and getting more hysterical by the minute.

'I'm going to have somebody take you aside so you can relax a bit.'

'I don't want to—'

'Mr Gallagher!' a voice shouted from behind them. 'Kenny David from the Morning Star. Can you confirm it was your other daughter Sharon who was murdered?'

Gallagher turned to him as the room went quiet.

'You snivelling little fuck. Who the fuck let you in here?'

'Is it true then?' David said, smiling.

For an older bloke, Gallagher could move. Or maybe it was just the adrenaline coursing through his veins that made him shift, but it was enough to wipe the smirk off the reporter's face.

Gallagher got a punch in, connecting with the man's jaw and knocking him sideways. David's face changed and, before Harry could get to him, he snarled at the older man and took a swing at Gallagher.

Gallagher ducked and the reporter's fist connected with Harry's nose, which knocked him off his feet.

Harry saw a blur of movement as Alex blocked another punch and body slammed the man to the floor before Robbie Evans was also on top of him followed by uniforms.

Harry felt himself being dragged away from the hustle and looked up to see Dunbar standing over him. Harry had tears coming from his eyes and blood out of his nose.

Stewards came running to help and the reporter was taken away by uniforms. Alex rushed over to him and knelt down beside Harry.

'You okay?' she said.

Harry could only nod his head for a second.

'This laddie's been in worse fights, I'm sure,' Dunbar said, turning to one of the stewards. 'Get a first aid kit, man! And towels. And get a fucking medic in here.'

Angus McPhee rushed across with a first aid kit from behind reception and knelt down. 'I was an army medic,' he said.

Harry groaned as the big man checked him over and stemmed the blood flow.

'You're going to be fine. You might have a shiner, but your nose isn't broken. I'll have paramedics check you over.'

'It's fine. I've had worse.'

Ten minutes went by and Harry started to feel better.

'I'll have that wee bastard arrested and charged with assaulting a police officer.'

'It's fine, Jimmy. It just got out of hand, that's all.'

'If this was fucking Govan...'

'You okay, sir?' Alex said.

'I'm fine. Good work. Your reflexes are okay, that's for sure.'

'Not bad for a wee lassie, eh?' She smiled at him.

'Thanks. But I have to call the team. I won't be long, Jimmy.'

'Take your time.'

'Come on, Alex, you can help me, in case my eyes start watering.'

'It wouldn't be the first time I made a man's eyes water.'

They walked upstairs to Harry's room. 'Maybe you should have a wee something from the mini bar,' she said as he closed the door behind them.

'A Milky Way?'

'Yeah, if that's what you want to call it.'

He got his iPad and FaceTimed Jeni Bridge. 'Start at the top and work our way down, I reckon.'

FIFTEEN

DC Simon Gregg got out of the car and grabbed his jacket from the back seat. 'Would it kill them to get cars with air conditioning?'

'They have air conditioning,' DI Karen Shiels said. 'It's called *rolling the window down*.'

At six feet six, Gregg was a big man, dwarfing Karen, but what she didn't have in stature, she made up for in attitude.

'How can it be this hot in Edinburgh? I read that it's going to be hotter here than in Rio. Can you believe that?' he said.

'You'll soon be complaining about the snow when it comes.'

'You've been working with me for too long.'

'You're stuck with me now, Simon. Now that we're part of Harry McNeil's team, I'm not going anywhere.'

'Did I ever show you how to thwart somebody if they go in for one of those crushing handshakes?' he asked as they walked up to the front door of the house in Dovecot Road in Corstorphine.

'That's why I don't shake hands,' she answered.

'I thought it was because you had hands like shovels.'

'Like you? You know what they say about a man with big hands, don't you?'

'They have a big heart?'

'Something like that.' She knocked on the front door, a bright yellow affair and took in the details of the detached house. It was old, a solid stone-built property that looked like it had attic conversions in the roof to create more rooms.

Finally, a young woman answered and both detectives held out their warrant cards for her to read.

'Mrs Dubois?'

'Miss Dubois. Sheila. Is there something wrong?'

'Can we step inside?'

She stood to one side to let them in and showed them into a room on the right. It was light and airy. Wood panels surrounded the bay window while a large-screen TV was opposite a comfortable-looking couch.

'Please, sit down,' Sheila said. 'It's not Vince, is it? Nothing's happened to him?' Karen shot Gregg a quick look before they took their seats on the couch, and waited until the woman sat on a chair.

'Can I ask your relationship to Vince?'

'I'm his sister.'

'It *is* about Vince, but we just need to ask you a few questions.' She looked at the young woman; unkempt hair, no make-up, wearing a baggy sweater. Karen didn't judge people but she always took a note of the way they were dressed.

'Is it about that damned wedding? I told him he shouldn't go. I saw it on the news this morning; that lassie's missing, isn't she?'

'If you mean, Marie, then yes. We're still looking for her.'

'Not you personally, of course, I take it,' the woman said.

'Our colleagues. But we'd like to know why Vince travelled up there.'

Sheila looked at them as if they were crazy. 'He was invited, that's why.'

Karen looked puzzled. 'Invited? By whom?'

The woman shook her head. 'That bloody trollop.'

'Marie Gallagher?'

'Yes, Marie bloody Gallagher. You would think it was bad enough that she dumped him for that other man, but to then invite him to attend the wedding? That was rubbing his nose in it.'

'Did he say why he wanted to go?' Gregg asked.

'He said, *at least it's a free meal.*'

'Have you heard from Vince at all?' Karen asked.

'Not since Friday. He let me know he had got there safely. Why? Is there something wrong?' she asked again.

'Not that we know of, but my colleagues want to interview him, and they keep missing him. He's been joining search teams.'

'That's my brother; generous to a fault. I would leave the lassie to rot.'

'You didn't get on with her?' Gregg asked.

'Oh, don't get me wrong, I got on well with her. Her family were nice, no complaints there. It was the way she dumped him. She accused him of having an affair and ended the engagement overnight.'

'*Was* he having an affair?' Karen asked.

The young woman sat back in her chair, like she was expecting an electric current to start shooting through it at any moment.

'He said no. That she was just being jealous, but she had already struck up a friendship with Duncan Randall. Vince said he thought Marie was just looking for an excuse to get out of marrying him. That she had found somebody better. Turns out, Duncan Randall was that somebody.'

'Does he have a girlfriend now?'

'He doesn't have a steady girlfriend. He's not ready to settle down after what happened with Marie.'

'Do you know if he went to the wedding with anybody?' Gregg said.

'Oh, no, he went on his own.'

'It must have stung, being treated like that and then being invited to watch his ex-girlfriend marry somebody else.'

Sheila shrugged. 'It was water under the bridge.'

'Can I ask what Vince does for a living?' Karen said.

'He's a video game designer.'

'That must pay well,' Gregg said.

'It does. This is his house. Bought and paid for. I live with him.'

Karen looked at the ornate fireplace, which appeared original and housed a gas fire. On top was a row of photos, all of them portraying a young man. Along with different women. One had been taken on a ski slope somewhere, with the sun shining. In it, Vince was smiling and the blonde woman next to him was showing off a set of perfect teeth.

There were another couple of photos of Vince and his sister.

Sheila saw her looking at the pictures. 'That was in better times. That's Marie with him on a trip to France. It's hard to believe that she turned out that way. He loved her. I still can't believe she married somebody else.'

'Do you have Vince's mobile number?' Karen asked.

'I do.' She fished her own phone out of her pocket and read the number off. Karen wrote it down then stood up. 'Thank you. You've been very helpful.'

Sheila let them out into the sunshine.

'It seems that Vince was up there legitimately. I'm going to give him a call. Why don't you get the car running and put the air conditioning on?' She made a *roll down the window* motion with her hand and took her phone out. She dialled in Vince Dubois' mobile number.

After a few seconds, it went to voicemail and she left a message to contact her.

When she got in the car, Gregg had the air conditioning going and Karen stuck her arm on the window edge.

'See? Now you're getting the hang of it.'

She smirked as she looked through the net curtains as the two detectives got back in the car, the mobile phone held up to her ear.

'It's me,' she said. 'There was a little problem at this end, but I took care of it.'

'What sort of problem?'

'Two detectives showed up when I was in the house. Don't worry, I took care of them.'

'They weren't suspicious?'

She laughed. 'Not at all.

'Be careful, for God's sake. We can't afford to blow it now. It's almost done.'

'I know. I'll be careful. The next part will be easy, and I'll have my little helper with me, so it should look convincing.'

'See you soon.'

'Yes, you will.' She disconnected the call and watched the police officers drive away.

SIXTEEN

'Tell me some good news, Harry,' Commander Jeni Bridge said. She was in her office, sitting on one of the lounge chairs near a coffee table.

'I wish I could, ma'am. It's not very good news at all.'

'Broderick Gallagher was on the phone to the chief constable this morning. And since the chief is my ex-husband, he felt the need to call me up and have a chat. He also knows what side his bread is buttered, so he said it in a nice tone. Apparently, Gallagher is being a Grade-A pain in the arse. He's going to let the chief have it the next time they're at the golf club together. Somehow, Gallagher thinks that we can wave a magic wand and solve the case.'

'That would be nice.'

'Since we both know that it's going to be good old-fashioned police work that will solve it and not a little boy wearing a gown, tell me what's going on.'

'We thought we had found the burning corpse of Marie Gallagher last night. I checked along at the mortuary this morning, and it turns out that it was the corpse of Gallagher's other daughter, Sharon.'

Jeni all but blew her coffee over her screen. 'What in the name of Christ do you mean?'

Alex leaned forward. 'Ma'am, we thought he had killed Marie and was playing games. He'd blown her head off with what we thought was a shotgun. There is no visual identity. We had been told Marie has pins in her arm after it was broken years ago, but the burned corpse didn't have any pins. That's when the mortuary technician showed us the tattoo. That's how we identified Sharon Gallagher.'

'Any sign of Marie?'

'No. We found the guide who had taken the group searching for Marie. Somebody had taken him and the three women, killed the guide, tied up the other two women and then took Sharon.'

'You told me that you want to talk to a man called Vince Dubois in connection with Marie's disappearance. How has that gone, so far?'

'He was spotted on CCTV here at the hotel, and he was last seen being dropped off at a gathering point for a search party. He hasn't been seen since. I asked

DI Shiels to go and talk with his mother in Corstor-phine. I'm still waiting for her to call me back.'

'Here's what I'm thinking, from what you've told me. Dubois was upset that he had been dumped, then attended the wedding, pretending to be a guest, then waited his turn and killed Sharon.' She sat back for a moment. 'Nah, that sounds all wrong. Why wouldn't he kill Marie? Why would he kill her sister?'

'Maybe he wanted to hurt Marie,' Alex said. 'There's been no sign of her, so we're starting to think he has her somewhere.'

'The problem is, we don't know where he would keep her,' Harry said.

'Couldn't he have just driven off with her? Put her in the boot of a car and driven out?'

'Ma'am, the press has been camping out for days, waiting to take a photo of Marie in her wedding dress. All the editors want to stick it to Broderick Gallagher because he banned the press from his daughter's wedding. It turns out that he's done a deal with a maga-zine. One of those society jobs, and they did the wedding photos. Outside the gates, it's a circus. There's no way Dubois would be able to drive out and nobody have a photo of him. Besides, one of the stewards dropped him off when they were gathering people to make up search parties, and that's the last they saw of him.'

'The magazine crowd didn't stick around to get a photo of her mutilated sister, I hope?'

'Apparently they've already left. They were going to do a follow-up with the honeymoon, and take photos of the couple in their first marital home. But the red tops are still out in force.'

'What's her new husband got to say about all of this?'

Harry had a quick sideways glance at Alex before answering. 'That's just the thing; we haven't spoken to him. DCI Dunbar has, but only briefly. Nobody's seen him since. He's been distraught and out looking for his wife.'

Suddenly, they heard shouting from outside the hotel room door. 'Ma'am, there's a ruckus going on again. I think we should go and see what's happening.'

'You haven't been fighting, have you, DCI McNeil?'

'There was a to-do with a reporter and I got in the way of his swing as he tried to hit somebody else.'

'You should learn to duck faster. It worked for my ex-husband.'

Jeni Bridge disconnected the call and Harry put his iPad away before they left the room.

He called Karen Shiels. 'How did things go at your end, Karen? I need to hear something positive.'

'Greggs have their Scotch pies on sale,' she said. 'If that helps.'

'It doesn't. But it's something to look forward to when I get home. Anything else?'

'We spoke to Vince Dubois' sister. He was up at the wedding because he was invited.'

Harry was quiet for a moment. 'Invited?' He looked across at Alex. 'Hold on, Karen, I'm going to put you on speaker here. I have DS Maxwell with me.'

'Hello, Alex.'

'Hi, Karen.'

'Right, so now we're all sitting round the campfire. Why would Marie invite her ex to the wedding? I mean, is that the done thing?'

'I'm not sure about that,' Karen said. 'I wouldn't invite my ex to my wedding, if I was getting married.'

'Me neither,' Alex said. 'I can't even imagine. Unless Marie's ego was so big, that this was her chance to rub Vince Dubois' nose in it. Like, *Look at me, loser. I'm marrying somebody else.*'

'To be honest, I didn't get that impression from his sister.'

Raised voices were coming from downstairs.

They rushed down the grand staircase and saw Terence Randall standing shouting at Broderick Gallagher again.

'Clean your fucking ears out! I said, this is all your

fault! Nobody's seen my son and I don't know where the hell he's gone to!'

'You should have been keeping an eye on him!' Gallagher spat back at him.

'If you had been keeping an eye on that hoor of a daughter of yours, my son wouldn't have got entangled with her. You and that toerag wife of yours. Barely older than your own daughter, you mucky old cunt!'

'Fucking jealous! I couldn't even get it up for that old washed-up boot you call a wife. At least I still have it in me to produce offspring!'

'If he really is yours! I bet he looks like the fucking milkman!'

It seemed that Gallagher had had enough of the word slinging and decided to make it physical. He threw a punch that landed on Randall's left cheek. The man fell down and skidded across the polished marble floor.

Several women screamed as stewards came running, Angus McPhee in the lead.

'Gentlemen! I know you own the hotel, but you employ me and my men to dispel any unruly behaviour. How about I start with both of you?'

He was glaring at Gallagher, who was standing, out of breath and rubbing his hand. Some of the kilted stewards were lifting Randall to his feet. They escorted him through to the back office where one of them mentioned he was going to get a first aid kit.

'I've not seen a right hook like that for a long time,' Harry said to Gallagher.

'Bastard deserved it.'

'That's not for me to judge, but why don't we go into the bar and relax a bit.'

Alex walked through with him as Jimmy Dunbar came running in through the front door. 'Evans told me there was a pagger,' he said, stopping and trying not to have a coronary in the hotel lobby.

'Hardly a pagger, Jimmy. Terence Randall got skelped by Gallagher, and now they're away to their corners, as it were.'

Dunbar's breath was still coming thick and fast. 'Jesus, that wee arsehole has a lot to answer for. I thought it was the razor wars starting up again. I'm going to kick him in the fucking goolies.'

'You would make a great phone perv with that breathing, Jimmy. Maybe you should make use of the hotel gym while we're here.'

'I'm going to make more use of the bar, let me tell you. *And* it will not be put on our bill, if Randall knows what's good for him. He still has to go back to Glasgow.'

'We should at least go through and get you a glass of water.' He clapped Dunbar on the shoulder as they headed to where Alex had gone with Gallagher. 'See? This is why I don't exercise.'

'My wife is always telling me I should go to the gym back home, but unless there's a bar called *The Gym*, I'm fine going to my local.' He looked at Harry. 'Don't let that woman of yours tell you otherwise, m'man.'

'Preaching to the choir, Jimmy.'

They saw Gallagher sitting at a table with an ice-filled bar towel wrapped around his hand. Alex sat close by as the barman brought over a whisky and a water for Alex. Harry asked him for another two waters.

'What in the name of Christ is going on here, Gallagher?' Dunbar said.

Gallagher looked at the policeman like he had lost his marbles. 'Excuse me?'

'You have one daughter who's been confirmed deceased, one missing, and now the new bridegroom is also missing. You might not have noticed, but we've got a lot on our plates here, without you two acting like a pair of daft wee laddies.'

Harry waited for the fireworks, but none came. 'You're right. I'm sorry. I should be mourning Sharon and trying to find Marie, but instead I'm bickering with that twat.' He looked at Harry. 'I never liked him. I grew up in Niddrie and made my own money.

Randall's father bankrolled him, and granted, he's made a bob or two, but he would be cleaning toilets now if it wasn't for his old man propping him up.'

'Let's try and keep calm about everything,' Harry said. 'It's not doing Marie any good, everybody in here going boxing when we should be focusing our energy on getting your daughter back.'

Gallagher couldn't argue with that.

SEVENTEEN

'How do I look?' Kerry Hamilton said, standing in front of the mirror in her office. It was always important to look good, no matter what you were doing.

'You might want to lose the cigarette,' Rose, her assistant, said. 'A ciggie bobbing up and down with ash flicking all over the place might not give the right impression.'

Kerry took the cigarette out of her mouth and stubbed it out. 'Clucking like a mother hen. Why *do* I put up with you?'

'Because you love me, you little toerag.'

Kerry turned and smiled. 'I do. I haven't heard from my own mother in years, so you'd better have aspirations of staying here for a long time.'

Rose saw the worry lines on Kerry's face and went over to give her one of what she called her *gentle hugs,* which was basically putting her arms around her without creasing the business suit.

'I'm not going anywhere.'

Kerry stood back and looked at Rose; the older woman was dressed in a business skirt and jacket, with a white blouse. 'You look perfect.'

'I look like an old dinner lady who's just won the pools.'

'*Lottery*, Rose, *lottery*. Who does the pools nowadays?'

'You know what I mean. Some daft old boot with money in the bank and not knowing how to spend it.'

'You're earning good money now because you've worked bloody hard for it. Don't you ever forget that, lady. And yes, there is a lot more where that came from. You're my right-hand woman now.'

Rose smiled. 'One thing is concerning me.'

'What's that?'

'This business with Marie Gallagher.'

Kerry smiled. 'It's all in hand. You said her mother called this morning and it's all a storm in a teacup.'

'That's not what the papers are saying. They're reporting that she's still missing.'

'You know what the tabloids are like. Besides, Broderick Gallagher owns *The Caledonian*. I heard he didn't allow any of the hacks to get into the hotel.'

'He did a deal with *Here Today* magazine,' Rose

said. 'They wanted exclusive access to the wedding, which they got.'

'And that's why the red tops are saying she's still missing! They want sensationalism. They'll write anything to make Gallagher look like a clown.'

'He is a clown.'

'A *rich* clown. Who do you think bought the honeymooners this new apartment along the road?'

Rose looked at her watch. 'Is that woman still coming?'

'If by *that woman* you mean Anne Gallagher, then yes, she's meeting us there. Gallagher himself wanted her to be there, to represent Marie and her new husband. To oversee everything. He has trust issues, that man. We could have handled everything perfectly for his little spoilt princess.'

They left the offices at the West End and climbed into Kerry's little Porsche Macan.

'See? I got rid of the nine eleven. Two low, indeed. Is this better for you?'

'It is, but let's see if you can do the two-minute drive without me reaching for a sick bag.'

She made it down to Haymarket Terrace and drove along to *The Rhind*, a fabulous design of apartments that was once a school for children. The development was named after famous Edinburgh architect David Rhind.

'You said the finishing touches were being put on the houses built round the back of the school,' Rose said, as the German car swept through the gates and up the driveway.

'Yes, they are. It's all interior work now. We're all going to make a bloody fortune out of this, Rose. You included.' She smiled as she turned the engine off.

They walked into the entrance hall of the building.

'You must be Kerry Hamilton,' a young woman said, approaching. She had a little boy with her.

'I am.'

'Anne Gallagher. This is my son, Rory. And my daughter's friend, Claire.'

Kerry smiled at the child, who was beginning to tug at his mother's arm. 'I'm so sorry to hear about your daughter. Has there been any news?'

'No. We're hoping it was just some kind of spat. Marie has always been very highly strung.'

They got to the top floor and Kerry led them along to an apartment door. 'This is the one you and your husband bought. I know you haven't seen it yet, but I'm sure you'll be just as impressed as he was.' She took out a key and let them in.

'He raved about it. And since it's for our daughter, he wanted the best.' The door was closed behind them.

It was a two-bedroom apartment with a small terrace.

After looking around, Anne seemed to be satisfied. 'It looks good. My husband would have been here in person, but he's still up north, waiting for any news. However, he instructed me to get the keys. Our daughter and her husband should be doing this, but I'm sure everything will work out. It's our gift to them and I can't wait to hand over the keys.' There were tears in her eyes and Claire stepped forward and put an arm around the woman for a moment.

'I was shocked when I heard the news, but I'm praying for a safe return for your daughter, Mrs Gallagher,' Kerry said.

'Thank you. Let's just hope she was overwhelmed by the wedding and is on a spending spree in London or something.'

They went back downstairs, Rory running ahead.

'Don't go too far, darling!' Anne shouted, but Claire got a hold of the little boy.

'Looks like somebody could do with a nanny,' Kerry said.

'You're telling me. But he's not our problem.'

'And to the Lord we are thankful.' They stepped out into the sunshine and watched as Anne Gallagher struggled to get her little boy into the big Range Rover while Claire got in behind the wheel. She didn't look in their direction as she sped away.

EIGHTEEN

Terence Randall came back into the bar and had a quick look around. He didn't see Broderick Gallagher anywhere, so he stepped up to the bar.

'Have you talked to your son?' Harry asked him.

Randall looked like a very old man now. He looked at Harry and slowly shook his head. 'I don't know where the hell he is.'

Dunbar looked at the man. 'What do you mean? Isn't he in his room?'

'I'd have said so, wouldn't I?'

'Have you tried calling him on his mobile?' Harry said.

'I did. When I went into his room. I heard it ringing and it was in a drawer in the nightstand.'

'Nobody goes anywhere without their phone

nowadays, especially the younger crowd,' Harry said, making himself feel like he was ancient.

'Aye, well, my son has. God knows where he is.'

Dunbar put a hand on Randall's shoulder. 'Get yourself a brandy, Terry. A stiff one.' He indicated for the barman to supply the drink. 'Is the room open?'

Randall nodded. 'Aye. I'm telling you, if he hurt that lassie, I'll give him a fucking good belting, let me tell you. Then you can throw the book at him.'

'Let's hope there's some reasonable explanation of why there's blood on his suit jacket,' Harry said.

'It looked like the bed had been made, then slept in a bit. Go up and have a look for yourself.'

Harry nodded to Dunbar and they left the bar and headed upstairs to the bridal suite where the bride and groom's rooms were, as well as the room where they would have been staying after they were married.

Harry gripped the door handle as if he was expecting an axeman to jump out at them, but it was all quiet. The bed was just as Randall had said; made, but looking like somebody had had a romp on it. Albeit a very quick romp.

'Pull the covers back, Harry,' Dunbar said.

Harry didn't argue and gingerly approached the bed as though there was a horse's head in it, although the lack of bump in the covers indicated otherwise. He pulled the quilt towards himself and looked down at the blood on the sheets.

'Jesus, what's that laddie got himself into?' Dunbar said.

'Are you thinking what I'm thinking?' Harry said.

'That he's a murdering bastard who's topped his wife and now he's hiding?'

'More or less.'

'Jesus, Harry, have we been looking in the wrong place all this time?'

'I'm beginning to wonder. I thought Duncan Randall was just grieving for his wife, and out helping to look for her, but all this time, he's possibly murdered her.'

NINETEEN

Claire Blythe sat in the driver's seat of the Range Rover and floored it towards Roseburn, heading back to the house at Barnton.

'Thank you for coming with me, and for staying with us,' Anne Gallagher said.

'That's what friends are for, Anne. You and I were friends before you met Broderick.'

'I know that.' She took in a breath and let it out slowly. 'My husband wanted security guards round the clock, but that's no way to live. I do feel safer with you here.'

'Safety in numbers. But I don't think we have to worry about Vince. To be honest, I didn't figure him for the jealous type, far less a murderer.

Anne reached over and squeezed Claire's hand. 'Marie thought a lot of you. I mean, she loved Sharon, of course, but sometimes you bond with friends more than siblings. You know what I mean?'

'I do.'

It didn't take them long to reach the big house. Claire clicked the button in the car that would open the electric gate and waited for it to open before driving through. She parked at the house, waiting until the wood-covered steel gate slid closed behind her.

She unlocked the car then walked round to the back to extricate the little boy from his car seat. It was hot outside, a big difference from the cooled interior of the car.

'You want to get some ice cream?' she said, smiling.

'Yes, please,' the boy said as she took him by the hand and walked up to the front door,

TWENTY

Harry felt a headache coming on. The thought of a millionaire's son topping his wife on their wedding night was the stuff of fiction, but there they were, the forensics crew fiddling about with their tools of the trade.

One of them had come over to him and confirmed it was human blood.

'Now we just need to find out who it belongs to, but that's not going to happen very quickly,' Dunbar said.

'We should see if the Inverness team have come up with anything.'

'Let's get back downstairs before Evans manages to burn the hotel down or something.'

'The laddie's doing well.'

'Compared to what, Harry? He's destined for traffic, so he is.'

By the time they got back down to the bar, Evans was sitting talking to Alex.

'There you are,' Dunbar said.

'Did you manage to calm the situation down, sir?' he said, not quite smirking.

'It was hardly the Highland Uprising, Evans. And I'm glad you find that funny. Your sense of humour will come in handy when you're seeing old women across the road with your lollipop.'

Just then, Tom Gunn and Eddie Lister came in, saw the group of police officers and were about to turn round when they decided a pint was in order.

'I'm telling you, we're the victims here,' Tom said as he approached Harry. 'But oh no, let's get them down to the station and give them a going over.'

'It was hardly a going over now, was it?' Harry said.

'Might as well have been. And you know those twats with their cameras were waiting outside the police station. Did somebody tip them off?'

'None of us did,' Dunbar said.

'Aye, well, somebody did,' Lister said. He ordered two pints.

Harry turned his back to the two men who were now standing further along the bar. 'One of my officers visited Vince Dubois' house today.'

'They find anything?'

'They spoke to his sister.'

'What did she have to say about things?'

'She said that Vince was invited up here.'

Tom walked up and stood between the two detectives. 'I heard you talking about Vince Dubois' sister. We've known him for years and there's one thing you should know about him.'

'What's that then?' Harry said.

'He doesn't have a sister.'

TWENTY-ONE

He drove the car down the long-disused track before coming to a halt in front of the property. Grass and weeds had sprung up, taking back what was rightfully theirs. Nobody tended the place now. It was only a memory, and a distant one at that.

The weeds had grown through the gravel parking area in front of the house and now the grass was knee high all around the abandoned place. He stood still, listening to the birds. He thought he could hear children's laughter if he concentrated hard enough. A dog barking, too. A black Lab. He expected to see it running round from the back of the house, but no dog appeared.

The window frames had been painted green a long time ago, as if the owner had wanted to camouflage the property, so the house would blend into the forest.

He stepped round the right-hand side of the house, his boots trampling the tall grass down. He had to push aside some thick branches from a small tree that had grown sideways as it had sought out sunlight.

He was carrying a large holdall but it was light.

The back door hadn't been touched, he was glad to see. But if it had, then he would have heard about it. He took out his key and unlocked the padlock.

The door opened silently. He'd oiled it well before this all started. Closing it quietly behind him, he walked through the gloom. The windows had been boarded up years ago and only slivers of light made it through the wooden slats.

The little torch was ample to guide him through the debris inside, but he had already cleared a path for himself a long time ago.

He climbed the stairs, making his way along to one of the bedrooms, the floor creaking, announcing his arrival.

'There you are!' he said.

The man struggled in the chair, the gag muffling his voice.

'Relax there. Why are you so antsy today?' He strode across to the man, took the knife out of the holdall and reached round to the back of the chair to cut the plastic cable ties. 'Same rules apply; you try anything stupid, and I'll kill you without breaking sweat. Don't be a hero. Understand?'

The man's head nodded. His hair was bathed in sweat. It was hot in the house, especially upstairs with no breeze filtering through the any of the boarded-up windows.

'Right, we'll get you through to the bathroom, so you can do what you need but I'll be right here. If you run, I'll cut your tendons so you'll never run anywhere again. If you try and hit me, I'll cut your thumbs off. You do believe me, don't you?'

The man nodded. He had to be helped to stand up straight. His muscles were stiffening. There was no way he was going to be running anywhere.

He tore the duct tape off the man's face. 'P-please let me go. I won't say anything. I don't even know who you are. I... can't identify you.'

'Go to the bathroom.' He didn't look down at the front of the man's trousers, knowing he had already soiled himself.

They shuffled out of the room and across the hallway to the toilet. He helped the man sit down. The smell was bad but it was fighting with the odour of decay. The house was dying on its feet, just like the man who was sitting on the toilet.

'Take a shower. The water's still running but it's only the cold, obviously. Clean up and get dressed in the clothes I brought you.' He fetched some soap and shampoo from the holdall.

He stood outside the bathroom door, listening to the water running before heading along to the other end of the hallway.

He opened the door and saw the woman sitting on the chair where he'd left her. Her head was slumped on her chest and he stopped to study her for a moment, watching her chest rise and fall.

'See what I have for you? You're going to be wearing it soon.'

He took the wedding dress out of the holdall and laid it on the bed. The dress was large and he'd struggled getting it in.

The drugs would be wearing off soon, so he knew he would have to get the other one out of the shower and dressed.

He walked back along to the other bedroom and laid out the clothes on the bed. He'd already made sure the sheets and covers were fresh.

The noise of the shower stopped running. He strode over and gave the man a towel. 'Dry quickly and get back to the bedroom.'

The man stood shivering and gratefully accepted the towel and started drying. His captor didn't leave the bathroom, instead positioning himself in the doorway. He didn't think his prisoner would try and escape.

He had been told what would happen if he tried anything. He wasn't in a position to fight his captor, but even if he did, the man was big and would easily beat the weakened man in a fight.

'Right. Get back to the room.' He watched as the man walked carefully in his bare feet; getting a splinter was the least of his worries. He had the towel wrapped round his waist and held onto it with one hand.

'Good. Now get dressed, but drink this. It's a protein drink. I don't want you getting dehydrated. If you do as you're told, you'll be out of here as soon as possible.'

The man drank the first cup, a thick, milkshake type of drink, then the second and third.

The added ingredients would keep his senses dulled and make him feel a little tired.

'Now, I'm going to tie you to the chair-'

'No, please don't.'

He looked at the victim. 'As I was saying, I'm going to tie you to the chair. Just for a little while. Then they'll be coming for you.'

'Then I can go home?' His voice was raspy, failing now as the drugs kicked in.

'Yes, you can go home.'

The prisoner dressed in the clean clothes. He made to sit back down on the chair but was led to a clean one. Once he was sitting, the man started to put cable ties round the supports but sensed movement behind him.

The bedroom door slammed shut and before he could get to the handle, the key was turned in the lock.

'Open this door!' he shouted, but there was no reply. He threw his shoulder against it, but it didn't budge. He himself had reinforced the door jambs, both round the lock and the hinges on the other side, to stop his prisoner from kicking the door down, if he should somehow wake up and start battering the door.

It didn't stop him from trying.

The holdall! He knew he had something in there that would take care of the door.

He turned round in the now darkened room and took the small torch out of his pocket and turned it on. He opened up the bag and took out what he needed.

TWENTY-TWO

They were in the library, a uniform guarding the door, all sitting round Harry's iPad.

'This is what it must have been like when they did the first moon walk,' Jimmy Dunbar said.

'Michael Jackson?' Robbie Evans said.

Dunbar turned to look at him. 'Boaby, if I hear another bloody word out of you while this tablet is open, I swear to Christ...'

Evans waited until Dunbar had turned away before looking at Alex, who was sitting next to him. He made a face behind Dunbar's back.

'Right, Harry, when you're ready, give the order.' He was sitting next to Harry while DI Barrett from Inverness sat on the other side. All eyes were glued to the small screen.

'I thought you watched the first moonwalk?' Evans said. 'You were old enough to see it.'

'For fuck's sake, Evans, shut your pie hole.' He looked at Harry. 'His Native American name is *Running with scissors*.'

Harry nodded. Looked at the screen, at Karen Shiels's face. 'DI Shiels, breach!'

She turned the view so that the team up in the Highlands could watch a uniformed entry team smash the lock on the front door of the house, the door crashing back against the hallway wall. Then an armed response team was the first in, and when the house was clear, a swarm of uniforms was inside, followed by the detectives.

'Nobody upstairs, ma'am.'

'Right, I'll leave a copy of the search warrant. Everybody listen up; tear the fucking place apart.'

They watched as if looking through Karen's eyes. She turned right into the living room, moving her phone around then walked up to the mantel piece.

'Christ, they're gone,' she said. 'The photos of Dubois and his sister. They're gone.'

'A young blonde woman, you said.' Harry looked closer.

'There are other photos too, with other women in them, but the ones that had his sister in them are gone. Just those. The others are still there, as you can see.'

'There must have been something incriminating in them. But why would she have kept them on display when you were in there?' Dunbar asked.

'She wasn't expecting us. Whoever she is.'

'Describe her to us again,' Harry said.

'She was dressed casually, and she was about thirty-ish, give or take. Blonde hair, slim build, medium size up top. She had the makings of a good-looking woman, with a bit lippy and clean hair.'

'Thanks, DI Shiels. Have a good look around. Call me when you're done.'

Harry disconnected the FaceTime call and looked at Dunbar. 'This woman pretends to be Vince Dubois' sister when my officers turn up. If she knew he didn't have a sister, why would she pretend to be his sister? I mean, she was taking a hell of a risk, knowing we would find out.'

'I don't think she cares, whoever she is. For some reason, she thought that would throw us off the scent.'

'Unless she panicked,' Alex said. 'I mean, there she is, in Vince's house for whatever reason, and then the police turn up. Maybe she just panicked and said the first thing that came into her head.'

'Or maybe she was stalling,' Evans said. 'She knew the story wouldn't check out but she didn't care. By the time we found out, she was away.'

'Good point,' Dunbar said. 'The question is, why is this woman protecting Dubois?'

'Maybe a girlfriend?' Harry said. But something told him it went deeper than that and they were being played.

TWENTY-THREE

Marie ran as fast as she could downstairs, hearing the maniac banging on the bedroom door. She didn't know he had reinforced it, didn't know it was designed to keep somebody in the room. All she knew was, there had been a key in the lock and she had closed the door and turned it.

He had been giving them stuff to drink, and she'd had no choice but to drink it because she had been so thirsty, but she'd woken up feeling disoriented. It had to be a date rape drug.

Her feet thundered on the stairs as she went down, first to the small landing where the stairs turned, then down to the ground floor, and across to the front door. There was no key in this lock, no windows to break, no loose panels to kick out.

She turned and ran back down a little hallway that

led to the back of the house. It was dark but not pitch black. She heard the banging intensifying upstairs, getting louder and louder. She ran, staggering against a wall, and through an old doorway that hadn't seen a door in many years.

Into the kitchen. It was dirty and mouldy and smelled awful. But it was lighter in here. She ran to the back door, grabbed the handle and turned it.

And the door opened.

Her heart was beating like a drum but she didn't hesitate for one second. She was out of the door and into... where? She realised she didn't know where she was but anywhere was better than being stuck in here with... him.

It wasn't full dark but the darkness would come down with a vengeance soon and she didn't have her phone with the little light in it.

She ran out into the overgrown garden, the noise from upstairs diminishing. The house was in the middle of a forest, tall trees closing in, blocking the sunlight so that everything was in shade.

She turned and had a look at the house. It was big and dirty, with the windows boarded over, including the window in the kitchen door that she'd just run through. Nobody was coming just now, but she guessed it wouldn't be long before he smashed the door down and came after her.

She kept on running, battering her way through the weeds and tall grass with her thighs. She had been dressed in dirty old jeans and a grubby tee shirt. Prickly bushes grabbed at her clothes but she shrugged them off, fuelled by adrenaline.

Then suddenly she was on an old path. It was rough going but not as bad as the garden had been. Which way? Left or right? Either way took her beneath canopies of trees. She couldn't see far into the woods.

She chose left and started running as fast as she could, but she was weak and soon started tiring. She slowed, trying to conserve her energy.

She turned to look back again.

There was nobody there.

She didn't see the prying eyes looking out at her from the top window of the house.

TWENTY-FOUR

'Any news?' Broderick Gallagher asked. He was back in the bar, resorting to drinking whisky.

'Nothing yet,' Harry said, keeping the information about Vince Dubois' phantom sister to himself.

Gallagher shook his head as if he was about to say something derogatory but then thought better of it.

He hadn't wanted any dinner. Time for eating later, when he was in his room. Alone. Where he could think about what he would do to Duncan Randall if it turned out he had killed Marie and Sharon. Terence first though. He was the man who had brought Duncan into this world, so he was ultimately responsible.

The thought pleased him.

He watched as Harry walked away, then moved over to a corner of the bar, one with big windows overlooking the grounds. Lights were on now, starting to light up the area surrounding the hotel. How could things have turned out like this?

He had decided to sell his share in this place. How could he ever enjoy it, after what had just happened?

He put his glass on the table and took his mobile phone out and dialled his wife's number. Hopefully, speaking with her would cheer him up.

TWENTY-FIVE

It was dinnertime and Alex had a little side salad sitting next to a dish that smelled good but looked awful. 'This case is getting twisted, Harry,' she said, poking at something green that looked like it may or may not be alive.

'It has to be related to Gallagher somehow. Sharon dead, his other daughter missing. Maybe a business deal gone wrong?'

'You don't get to his position without stepping on a few toes.'

'What's that you're eating, anyway?' He put a piece of beef into his mouth and chewed, pointing at her dinner with his fork.

'Beef Bolognese.'

'Really? I thought you were more a mince and tatties kind of girl.'

'You saying I'm chunky?'

'Not at all. Just... built for fun.'

She looked at him for a moment, not sure how to take his comment. 'You do see the salad there, don't you?'

'Camouflage, that's what that is.'

'Listen to Johnny Two Pies.'

'I can handle it. My mother always said I burn fat off like nothing on earth.'

'Ah, a mother's love. Looking at her wee boy through her love goggles.'

Harry's phone buzzed about on the table. He saw Vanessa's name pop up and wondered if he should answer it. Then it stopped and a message came up saying he had a voicemail.

'I would think before you answer it, sir,' Alex said. 'You don't want to show her you're too keen.'

'How did you know it was Vanessa?'

'Duh. I can read upside down.'

'Is there no end to your talents? Don't answer that.' He picked the phone up and listened to the message. Then he put the phone back down.

'If you want a woman's opinion—'

'I don't.'

'Let me finish. If you want a woman's opinion, you'd be better off letting her stew. It doesn't matter why she called you, just the fact she did means she wants to communicate. If you call her, the next thing you know, you'll be running back to her, and then she'll have won. And then it's game over, Harry, I'm telling you.'

'She just wanted to let me know that all my stuff is in boxes now and she's leaving them outside my door.'

Alex poked at some salad. 'Okay. That was my second choice.'

'Your female intuition is needing a little tune-up.'

'No, no, that's not it at all. I stand by what I just said. Now, if she really wanted to end it, she wouldn't have done anything with your stuff. Trust me, Harry. This is her attention seeking. If you want her, call her. Explain things. Tell her you'll be round to pick them up and then she'll talk to you. But if you think it's over, then don't call her.'

He ate some more beef. 'I already sent a text to my next-door neighbour. She'll look out for the boxes.'

'Good man. I'm proud of you.' They ate in silence for a moment. 'Where's Jimmy?'

'DCI Dunbar to you.'

'Really? We're doing this again? I can't call a senior officer by his first name?'

'No you bloody well can't.' His voice started to get higher and the other guests looked across for a moment. 'Sorry. My blood pressure got up a bit there.'

'Duly noted, DCI McNeil. I will never call you Harry again.'

'You're kidding, right?'

'Yes, Harry.'

'I knew it was too good to be true.'

She washed down her salad with some water. 'Seriously, where did Jimmy get to?'

'I haven't a clue. Evans is doing his nut in. I'm glad I don't have an annoying sergeant with me.'

'That would be tragic.' She looked at him. 'Oh, I see; that was sarcasm.'

Harry finished off his plate. 'I don't think there's going to be anything more we can do tonight. Vince Dubois is still giving us the runaround.'

'And let's not forget Duncan Randall. Do you suppose Randall caught Marie and her ex in an embrace and he let them both have it?'

'I'm not ruling anything out. But these damn forests go on forever.'

'You should mention that to management. I'm sure they can use that in their next brochure.'

Despite himself, Harry grinned. 'I want a commission.' He sat back. One of the waiters came over and took their plates away returning with a coffee carafe.

'Thank you,' Harry said after the coffees were poured. Then he caught the waiter's attention again. 'I have a question.'

'Go ahead, sir.'

'The stewards that work here. Who hired them?'

'The management.'

Harry nodded.

'Oh, and Angus McPhee had a say, too, since he was the one who recommended some of them.'

'How long have they worked here?'

'Since the hotel was bought by Mr Gallagher and Mr Randall, sir. About six or seven months, like a lot of us here.'

'Do you have much interaction with them? Meaning, do you know them well?'

'We work with them, but I don't know anybody who socialises with them. They live in the barracks that were built for them on the property so they don't have to travel to work, and they do shifts, so somebody is available twenty-four hours.'

'Okay, thank you.'

Alex waited until he was away before speaking. 'What was that all about?'

'I'm just wondering how a trained soldier let himself be taken like that steward Andy, was.'

'Look at the surroundings; woods, overgrown bushes and long grass. Anybody could get lost there. Just because he was a soldier, doesn't mean he couldn't be taken by surprise.'

'I know, but by somebody like Vince Dubois? A

desk jockey? The only gun he's fired is a virtual one, as far as we know.'

'He's crafty, Harry, and very cunning. Plus, he's got one of the shotguns and plenty of ammo.'

They finished their coffees then Harry threw his napkin onto the table and stood up. 'Come on, sergeant, let's go and talk to somebody.'

TWENTY-SIX

The track seemed to go on forever, meandering through the woods. She thought she should have come to a road by now, but nothing. Where the hell was she? Maybe she should have gone the other way, but it was too late now.

She felt the cramp in her stomach kick in. It had been there when she woke up earlier but it had subsided. Now it was back again. She stopped running for a moment, thinking it was maybe this that was causing her discomfort. But cramps were nothing compared to what the lunatic might do to her if he came after her.

She started running again. Marie thought about Duncan, and how they should have been going on honeymoon and coming back to their new apartment that her dad had bought them. Now, here she was, in the woods, trying to escape the clutches of a crazed killer.

She didn't know how long she had been running, but the sun was slowly going down and she had to find something before nightfall. Which looked like it was just round the corner.

She kept on going, and then she saw it in the distance: a road. The trees thinned out here and it was like a clearing or something. It wasn't a paved road, but it was a proper track, leading to... where? It had to be to civilisation.

The path she was on stopped at the road, which seemed to be going east to west, if the lowering sun was anything to go by. It was tucking in behind hills in the distance, so that meant that the house was on her left, way back.

Then she saw it; headlights coming! Jesus, she couldn't believe it. She ran into the middle of the road and jumped up and down, waving her arms. It was a Land Rover, and she thought it could be one belonging to the hotel. Why would anybody else be out here?

That was it, they were out looking for her. And one of them had found her. She was blinded by the full beam headlights for a moment, putting her hands up to shield her eyes.

Then the Land Rover was pulling up alongside her and the passenger window wound down.

'I'm Marie Gallagher! The woman you've been looking for!' As her eyes adjusted a little, she could make out the hotel's logo on the door. She felt such relief as the driver unlocked the door and she climbed in.

'You're in safe hands now, ma'am,' the bearded steward said. 'I'll get you back.' He continued driving in the direction he had already been going.

'Aren't you going to turn back?' she said.

'The main road's this way.'

'I think that's where the house is where I was being kept.'

The big car drove along the track with ease.

'The lodge house, or the gatehouse?'

'It was big.'

'That'll be the lodge house. Great big dirty thing?'

'Yes. Looks like a haunted mansion. You know it?'

'Aye. I'm pretty sure it was checked out already, but maybe they thought nobody was in there because it was boarded up.'

Marie was excited, relieved, but she also felt the anger kicking in. Why the hell hadn't somebody gone into the house to check? To damn well make sure?

They rounded a corner and the house came into view.

'There it is!' Marie shouted. 'My husband is in

there! Can you call the police? I locked the guy in a room.'

The Land Rover stopped right at the door.

'I can do better than that,' the steward said. He reached round the back of the seat and pulled out a shotgun. Marie was hesitant to step out but she didn't want to let the man out of her sight.

He had switched the headlights off and now the darkness enveloped them, but her eyes started to adjust to the gloom.

'Where is your husband?'

'Upstairs. Turn left. There's a door on the left with a key in the lock. Please be careful.'

The man smiled, his white teeth showing through his beard. She'd never thought she would be so happy to see a man in her life. She knew the stewards were all ex-army, so her captor was going to be up against a former soldier.

He walked up to the front door and turned the handle, and the door opened silently. The steward lifted the shotgun up to his face then he turned round to Marie.

'You need to wait here. But tell me what he's wearing.'

'He always had a ski mask on. Wearing water-proofs. Jacket and trousers, with a hood.'

'Even inside?'

'Yes.'

'Right. Leave him to me. Scaring a wee lassie like that, the bastard.'

'Oh God. Please be careful,' Marie said, ignoring the remark about her being a wee lassie.

'I will. If he tackles me, he'll know all about it.' She watched as he walked into the hallway, then climbed the stairs to the first landing, before continuing to the foot of the second staircase and disappearing from sight.

Marie looked all around her, but everything was dark. Please let Duncan be alright, she prayed.

Then she heard the shotgun go off.

TWENTY-SEVEN

Jimmy Dunbar had appeared after dinner and sat with Harry at a table while Evans was up at the bar with Alex.

'He's as good as a man short,' Dunbar complained.

'At least he's putting his hand in his pocket.'

'That's his one redeeming feature. What about that lassie you're here with?'

'She's proving to be a good detective, to be honest.'

'Don't let her go anywhere, then. They're hard to come by.'

The two sergeants came back from the bar with the drinks.

'Cheers,' Harry said, taking a sip from his pint. The bar was quiet and there was no sign of either Gallagher or Randall.

'It's nice to relax a little bit,' Alex said. 'I felt guilty standing up at the bar when there's a woman and her husband still missing. I know one of them might be a killer, but I wish we had more of a lead.'

'Sometimes leads can come in thick and fast, other times, things go dry very quickly.'

'I told her not to be daft,' Evans said. 'We can't be on duty all of the time.'

'Jesus, that's twice you've made sense since we came here,' Dunbar said. 'I'll need to mark it in the calendar.'

Evans gave his boss a look that could have either meant *thanks, sir* or *cheeky sod*.

'Oh, heads-up, here's Harry's new fancy piece,' Alex said with a grin.

They all looked at the doorway to the bar.

'What's this? Playing away from home?' Dunbar said with a grin.

'Give it a rest.' He shot Alex a look as Angie Patterson looked around the bar and saw them all. She walked across to them.

Harry stood up. 'Hello again. I didn't recognise you at first.'

'Didn't recognise me with my clothes on? My work clothes, that is.' She smiled. 'It's a joke.'

Jimmy stood up. 'I'm DCI Jimmy Dunbar and the young man who is about to get you a drink is DS Evans.'

She nodded. Then smiled at Alex. 'Hello again.'

Evans got up and took her order and she sat down, putting her handbag at her feet.

'So, Miss Patterson, I take it this isn't a social call?' Harry said.

'Correct. I came looking for you.'

Alex raised an eyebrow at Harry but he ignored her. Evans came back with the Coke. 'I'm driving,' she said by way of explanation.

'We're just comparing notes,' Dunbar said, as if he was worried she'd think they were well on their way to getting blootered.

'I was almost given a hard time by one of the uniforms guarding the gate. Those newspaper reporters were shouting at me, asking questions. I felt like royalty or something.'

'It was worth the barrage of questions just to have a drink with your favourite copper,' Alex said.

'Indeed it was. But I'm actually glad I can talk to you all.' She took a sip of her drink first. 'I got to thinking about Sharon Gallagher, as they came for her and the other victim today. I mean, they will have to go the extra mile to get an identification of the steward, considering his head was taken off with what we believe to be a shotgun.'

'They can do DNA from his family,' Dunbar said.

'It just sent a shiver down my back, considering

what happened all those years ago. It brought back a lot of memories.'

The detectives looked at her, waiting for her to go on. 'You know, the other shootings?'

'What shootings?' Harry asked.

'Fifteen years ago. When the man shot his wife dead and blew his own head off in front of his kids.'

'We don't know anything about that.' Harry looked at the others and they all shook their heads. 'Tell us about it.'

'I was fourteen at the time. I was friends with the family. And Doreen in particular of course. She went home from school one day and found her mother dead in the bedroom, shot by their father. Her brother, Michael, came home, and when he went upstairs, they were all in the parents' room. Doreen sat petrified on the bed and their father put the gun under his chin and pulled the trigger. Apparently, it was a sawn-off shotgun.'

'That happened here?' Dunbar said.

'Yes, here in town.'

'Do they know why he did it?' Alex asked.

'Because Edward, their father, was accused of abusing and killing two little boys. He was persecuted by the press. Doreen was hounded and they were bullied in school. Finally, they were taken out of school and they left.'

'So he thought he would kill his wife and then himself instead of going to prison?' Evans said. 'I don't blame him.'

'It couldn't have been easy for them,' Harry said.

'That's not all,' Angie said. 'It was a month later...'

TWENTY-EIGHT

Michael sat on the settee in the living room, watching the woman's TV. He didn't think of it as *his* TV, but the woman they were forced to live with now. She wasn't bad, despite all the horror stories they'd been told. *They'll kick your head in* or *you'll be given the belt for not eating your greens.*

But the woman was okay with them. She didn't take any shit, but she was fair, and the husband liked football, so they went to the match sometimes. Doreen was having a harder time than he was, but he reassured her he would look after her.

It was a Saturday afternoon that he found out his father wasn't a child molester. Michael was sitting watching TV when it was announced that police had arrested a man in connection with abusing several boys. He'd admitted to murdering the boys that Michael's father had been accused of killing.

Michael cried that Saturday evening. His father killing his mother and then taking his own life had all been for nothing.

The woman they lived with had spoken to the police who had told her that it was early days, and they would have to investigate further, but it was looking likely the man was telling the truth. He knew too many details that had been kept out of the press.

Michael's sorrow turned to anger as he looked at the face of the man on the TV and hated him with every fibre of his being. The man was a schoolteacher! He even knew Michael's dad, and he was also a football coach in his spare time, and the two boys were on the team he coached.

Then he read the report in the papers.

The teacher said he had abused the boys, who were then going to tell their parents but the teacher couldn't have that. He'd be ruined! He was a pillar of the community. He was a father to two little boys. What would people think? That he had touched his own two boys? No, he couldn't have that. It was an illness he had. He wasn't really a bad person.

At first, the teacher had spoken to the boys, told them he was a scout leader. They were going camping and he was coming along as a leader. They were at school, and they seemed daunted by the teacher talking to them about going on the camping trip, but when they saw him in his scout uniform, he was just another one of the boys.

They had a good time that weekend. They seemed pleased to see him in school, so they were more excited about the second trip they were going on. This time, he had invited them round to his tent. He'd exposed himself and began touching them.

He said they were frozen with fear. Afterwards, he told them not to say anything and he would give them drink round at his house. He invited them over the following weekend when he knew his wife was going to be out with his own boys.

They said they weren't coming round. In fact, one of them said he was going to tell his mother. The teacher promised them a lot of money. They just needed to meet him to collect it, and then they would never talk of it again.

He drove in his car to the waste ground, the boys arriving on their bikes.

He killed the first one with a hammer behind some bushes. The other boy didn't know his friend had been killed.

The teacher came out and shouted for him to come over and help his friend. He was ill.

As the second boy got closer, he saw the teacher

holding a hammer and he ran. He was fast, but not fast enough to outrun the man.

He'd just made it to his bike when the hammer caught him on the shoulder. He screamed and fell down. Then the teacher stood above him, looking down. He apologised then he brought the hammer down again, this time on the boy's head.

The teacher had rented a van and taken the boys bodies in the back of it and had driven onto the estate after dark and along the track then dumped the boys where they would be easily found.

He then took a blood-covered sweater and put it into the Land Rover that the coach drove for his work around the estate.

The following day, he had gone to a phone box and made an anonymous tip after the boys had been reported missing. Unbelievably, neither of the boys had told their parents where they had been going. It was only a matter of time, the teacher thought, so he felt relieved to have taken care of the problem when he had.

The police had gone to the estate and had asked Michael's father if they could search his Land Rover. He had agreed, thinking it strange they should be looking at his car, but they had come back with the sweater.

He had been arrested, but he had employed a

lawyer, who argued anybody could have put it there since the coach didn't drive the Land Rover exclusively and it wasn't kept locked at night.

Michael's father walked, but the police kept him as suspect number one and they came back with sniffer dogs.

The following day, they found the two boys.

Michael's father knew they would crucify him, that he would be found guilty by the court of public opinion.

He drove to the house, waited for the kids to come home then shot himself after shooting his wife.

The teacher thought he'd got away with it. And he would have if his *illness* hadn't taken over. He touched another little boy at scout camp but this little boy told his dad, who went looking for the teacher and caught him in the showers in the park pavilion after a football training session, and saw him touching another little boy.

Although tempted to batter the man, he called the police instead.

The teacher confessed to touching the boys and to murdering the other two lads.

Michael watched the reporter on TV telling the world that his father had been innocent after all.

A week later, the teacher hanged himself in prison while he was awaiting trial.

'And this happened locally, you said, Angie?' Harry said.

'Yes it did.'

'Near here?' Dunbar asked.

'Not *near* here – *here*. On the estate that Gallagher and his friend bought. They're adding it to this estate to make this place vast. The old estate fell into disrepair after the murders and the old man who owned it abandoned it. The mansion house was set on fire. The police think it was some vengeful locals, but nobody was ever caught, and the place fell apart. Until Gallagher bought it.'

'Show us,' Harry said.

TWENTY-NINE

Marie was shaking. It wasn't from the cold that had descended from the night sky, but fear. Total and utter fear. The steward hadn't come back to say he had taken care of the crazed killer and rescued her husband.

Shouldn't he be back by now?

She knew the sensible thing to do was to go and get help, so that is what she would do. She ran round to the driver's side of the Land Rover and got in.

The driver had taken the key.

Of course he had! Why did she think this would be easy?

She got back out, adrenaline coursing through her now. Of course, she wasn't armed but the steward was. She walked into the hallway, her eyes adjusting to the gloom. It was dark but the stairs could still be seen. She didn't shout out to the man. This was dangerous of course. What if she took him by surprise and he shot her? He had obviously shot at something.

Maybe he was trying to free Duncan. Yes, that had to be it. He was ex-army, and probably knew how to do this fighting in houses stuff.

She took the first step and started walking upstairs. She couldn't believe she was actually here, back in the house from where she had escaped only a little while ago.

The first landing was reached. She turned and took each step slowly until she reached the landing. God, she wished she had her phone right now, just for the little light.

Marie turned left and walked along the hallway. The bedroom door was open, the one she had locked. The wall next to the door jamb was smashed as if somebody had taken a hammer to it.

No, not *somebody*: the killer.

She inched along, expecting the man to jump out but nobody did.

Then she saw Duncan on the bed, his wrists tied to the bed frame by cable ties. He was looking at her, fully awake, but the tape over his mouth was preventing him from speaking.

Marie couldn't move. Not at first, but she steeled herself. *Just go in, cut the plastic ties somehow and get*

Duncan free. Then she saw the shoes, and then the socks. On somebody lying on the floor.

Oh God, no, please.

She inched further into the room and looked round the door. A steward was lying face down, his kilt up above his knees.

She was about to turn and run when the steward who had driven her here appeared behind her.

'Marie,' he said.

She gasped, her heart hammering. 'Oh thank God!' She looked at the man on the floor. 'Is that... the man who kept us here?'

He grinned at her, the shotgun pointing towards her midriff. 'I'm afraid not. You see, when you got out, I smashed my way out and drove round the other track and came out ahead of you, so it would look like I was coming from the hotel. I took off my waterproof gear so you would think I was one of the stewards. Now, get back in the room, put your wedding dress on and get on the bed with your husband.'

Marie's breath left her body as she froze. This couldn't be happening. But it was. This was very real.

'Who's that lying on the floor?' she asked.

'One of the other stewards I brought here a little while ago. He was in the other room, unconscious. He's part of the plan. He just didn't know it.'

THIRTY

They went in two Land Rovers, the armed officers in the front. It was decided they would drive through the estate. If the press saw them leaving, it was inevitable that somebody would follow them and then they would have civilians in the way and none of them wanted that.

'I don't understand what all of this has to do with Broderick Gallagher,' Evans said to Angie.

She was sitting in the back with strict instructions not to move from the car. She was to show them where the house was, and that was it.

'I haven't a clue,' she said. 'But I'm sure a young detective like you will be able to figure it out.' She smiled at him in the dark of the vehicle.

Harry looked at Alex sitting next to him in the

middle seats. 'Don't get all jealous now,' she said in a low voice.

'Just when I thought me and Angie could make a go of it.' he said.

A uniform was following behind the lead car, both vehicles driving with just their sidelights on. 'I hope he knows where he's going,' Dunbar said.

'You can't miss it,' Angie said. 'This track leads right into the parking area for the house then a few hundred yards further on, you come to the main road. There's a small gatehouse there, but that's been abandoned for years too.'

The lead car slowed down and so did theirs.

'We're here, sir,' the driver said, keeping well back.

The Reynolds house Angie had told them, *where Reynolds had shot his wife and then himself.*

There were nine men in the front car, all of them armed to the teeth. They got out and pointed their guns at the windows, some men holding back to cover the men who were going in.

Harry glanced at his watch, before looking out of the windscreen. They could only see part of the house from where they were, but their driver was ready to swing the car round and drive away at speed.

After ten minutes, an officer with a torch walked towards them and waved the driver forward. He drove up and they piled out.

'We've checked the house out, sir,' he said to Dunbar.

'And?'

'And it's not a pretty sight.' He led them forward into the house. They all switched their torches on, the multiple beams cutting through the darkness of the house.

He led them upstairs and they saw the body lying on the hallway floor, his head completely blown off. He was one of the stewards from the hotel, dressed in the kilted uniform.

'Who's that?' Evans asked.

Harry went through one of the pockets and pulled out a wallet. 'Angus McPhee,' he said. 'The head steward.'

'Christ, he went mental with a shotgun to blow his head completely off,' Dunbar said. 'I don't think Dubois is going to go down without a fight.'

'Maybe he was searching this place and the killer got him. Jesus.'

'You'd better have a look in there, sir,' the officer said, pointing with his own torch. The other marksmen were in the hallway but two of them were in the room.

They don't want to contaminate the crime scene, Harry thought. He stepped forward along with Dunbar and they looked into the bedroom.

Marie Randall, nee Gallagher and her husband

Duncan, were dressed in their wedding outfits, lying on the bed, side by side. Each of them had massive gunshot wounds to their fronts. They were both clearly dead but the officer confirmed it.

'I'm not a pathologist, but it's clearly shotgun wounds they have, and it's around where their hearts are. Death would probably be instant.'

Harry nodded. 'We'll have to tell Gallagher and Randall that their children are dead.'

'I wonder why he didn't blow their heads off like the others?' Dunbar said.

'Simple, Jimmy. He wanted to make sure we identified them right away.'

'We thought it might be Duncan Randall, but it was Vince Dubois all along,' Evans said.

'Don't say that to Terence Randall. We need to clear out and get forensics in here right away,' Harry said. 'Officer, stay here with your men, just to make sure. Post a couple outside, and a couple round the back. Make sure they're safe. We're going back to the hotel to break the news.'

'Yes, sir.'

The detectives led Angie outside into the cool night air.

'You were very helpful.'

She smiled at him. 'Glad I could be of help.'

He was about to get back into the Land Rover when he stopped.

'What is it?' Alex asked.

'Look around you. What *don't* you see?'

Alex had a look around the area in front of the house. 'Angus McPhee would have driven here. There's no car.'

'Vince Dubois shoots everybody in the house, and then takes the keys to McPhee's Land Rover, then where does he go to hide?'

'McPhee's apartment. It's on its own above one of the garages where the golf carts are kept.'

Harry issued orders to the firearms team and then they headed back to the estate.

There were several buildings in a clearing not too far from where the brand-new lodges had been built. The garages held the golf carts that the guests could use, which was recommended, as cars weren't normally allowed to use the tracks through the woods.

Angus McPhee, being the lead steward, had his own apartment above one of the garages. Stairs were on the outside, on the left-hand side of the building.

There was a Land Rover parked at the foot of the steps. Nobody else would park there, except McPhee.

Two firearms officers led the team up the steps. The door was open, and then they were inside, followed by the rest of the team.

Less than a minute later, one of the officers came back out and waved for the detectives to join him.

'He's here.'

'Alive and in handcuffs?'

The officer shook his head. 'Come and have a look for yourself.'

The lights had been switched on and they walked into the apartment and saw Vince Dubois, sitting on the floor in the bedroom, hands tied behind his back with a ligature round his neck, tied to a door handle. He was obviously dead.

'I wonder why he chose to come here and kill himself, instead of just doing it in the house where he had killed the others?' Alex said.

'We'll never know. At least we don't have to worry about a manhunt now.' He looked at her. 'Let's go and break the news to the families.'

THIRTY-ONE

Terence Randall and Broderick Gallagher were in the same room together and no fists had been flying.

'Is it Marie?' Gallagher said. He had been sleeping and his eyes were puffy.

'Yes, it is. And Duncan. I'm sorry to tell you both that we found them both. Deceased,' Harry said, and he waited for the outburst, but none came.

Randall started crying and Gallagher sat with his mouth open, saying nothing. There were family liaison officers from Inverness in the room and they went to sit beside both men. More uniforms were in the room, and DI Barrett from Inverness was standing back.

'How?' Gallagher suddenly said, brushing the FLO aside. 'How did she die?'

'That will be up to the pathologist to decide, sir,' Harry said.

'Don't mess me around, McNeil. You saw her, I want to know.'

'Me too,' Randall said, sniffing and wiping his eyes.

'It looks like they were both shot dead with a shotgun,' Harry said.

Gallagher stared into space for a moment before looking up at Harry. 'Both my girls were killed by a shotgun? Have you any idea who did this?'

'All we can say is, there was another person found at the scene, also deceased.'

Gallagher stood up. 'Just tell us. We're going to find out anyway, for God's sake.'

Harry looked across at Dunbar, who gave a nod of his head. 'It was Vince Dubois. He'd also killed one of the stewards up at the house before going elsewhere to commit suicide.'

'Vince? The one who was engaged to my Marie?'

'Yes, the same one.'

'Christ. The little bastard. He couldn't have her, so nobody could, is that it?'

Dunbar stepped forward. 'It's not like he gate-crashed. He had an invitation. We were told he was invited and my sergeant found his name on the guest list. We saw him on CCTV, so he was definitely here at the hotel.'

'Maybe he approached her when she was upstairs getting changed,' Randall said. 'I mean, nobody would have questioned him if he was walking about and he didn't look out of place.'

'Bastard. Who knew he was such a maniac?' Gallagher shook his head. 'I don't suppose I can see my Marie?'

'Not yet. Forensics are making their way to the scene and they'll be there all night. Then she'll be taken to Inverness for the PM. Then she'll be released, but I think you'll be able to see her at the mortuary.'

He sighed deeply. 'You know, I think I'll wait. I'll have my Anne with me. We will have to arrange the funerals for both girls. Randall can do what he likes, but I don't want to look at Marie in a smelly mortuary. I'm going to fly home in the morning when my jet gets back up here.'

He walked away out of the bar.

Randall stood up. 'I agree with him. I don't want to see my boy lying on some trolley, covered in a sheet. I'll see him back in Glasgow.' He also walked out of the room.

'It must be tough, being a detective at times,' Angie said to Alex.

'We both deal with dead bodies. Just in different forms. We get to see them first, then you deal with them.'

'Well, not me so much, but the pathologists.'

'This is the end of it, then, Harry?' Dunbar said.

'You would think so.'

'You got some doubts there, my friend?'

'Oh, it's nothing, Jimmy. Maybe I'm just over-thinking things.'

'I'm going upstairs to write my report. We'll be leaving tomorrow after breakfast, but I'll call my Super tonight.'

'Me too. I'll catch you tomorrow, Jimmy.'

'I don't know about you, but this feels anti-climactic,' Angie said after Dunbar and Evans had gone. 'I mean, I know I'm not part of your team, but—'

'You acted like you were a part of the team. You told us about the house, Angie,' Harry said.

'I wish I was coming down to Edinburgh. I'm bored out of my skull, working at that tiny hospital.'

'I'll keep my eyes and ears open. If a position opens up at the mortuary in Edinburgh, would you consider it?'

'I certainly would.'

'Give me your mobile number and I'll put you in my contacts.'

Angie gave it to him. 'Thanks, Harry. I'll head off home now. Hopefully you won't forget me.'

He smiled at her. 'After tonight? I won't forget you.' He watched her walk out of the room.

'Smooth talker. That was almost like the ending of a Humphrey Bogart film.'

'*Of all the murder enquiries...*'

'Don't give up your day job.'

'You're not jealous are you? That old Uncle Harry still has it in him to attract a younger woman?'

'I'm not the one you have to worry about, Harry. And you damn well know that Gus Weaver has retired from the Edinburgh city mortuary. *If a position comes up.* Are you going to put in a good word for her?'

'Of course not. I'll just let her know. Time we headed up as well.'

'Goodnight, Alex,' he said as they reached his room.

He watched her walk along the hallway to her room before going in to his own, then sat down on the edge of his bed. Instead of feeling tired, he felt wired. He knew he should maybe call Vanessa. Truth be told, he missed her. He took his phone out and was about to dial her number, when there was a knock at his door.

He debated whether to pick up the poker but decided not to bother as he opened the door.

Alex was standing looking at him.

'You really need a boyfriend,' he said.

'Why? I have you, don't I? But let me in, I want to talk to you about something.'

He stood by and let her in.

'If this is about you drinking on duty, I'll put in a good word for you,' he said to her.

'I think I'm the more sober one, don't you?'

'Not really, and I don't want to rush you, but can you say what you've come to say? I need to make a phone call.'

'Sounds like rushing to me. But I'm just having a hard time getting my head round this. Obviously, it looks wrapped up. Ex-lover of bride turns up at the wedding, and kills the bride and her new husband in a jealous rage. That's how the papers will see it. But there's something wrong.'

'Like?'

'Like, why did he pick that old lodge house to kill them in? More to the point, how did he know about it? And why was Angus McPhee there without anybody knowing about it?'

'Maybe he was just checking it out and was in the wrong place at the wrong time.'

She sat on a chair while he sat on the bed. 'I just got to thinking; we were told that the camera up in the bridal suite wasn't working. That was convenient. But if Vince Dubois was up there and was seen, somebody might have said something, despite what Randall thinks. But there is one person who could have floated about up there and nobody would have questioned him.'

'A steward.'

'Correct.'

'We've both dealt with murder cases before, and we've seen plenty of people try to cover up their crime, but not Vince. He was seen on CCTV, he accepted the invite, he got McPhee to take him to a group that were going out on a search.'

'Maybe he didn't care anymore. The love of his life was getting married to another man and he was at the end of the road.'

'Maybe. It just stinks, that's all.'

'We'd better get some rest,' Harry said. 'We have to drive back tomorrow and I still have those calls to make.'

'See you in the morning,' she said as she left the room.

Harry waited until he was sure she was really away. Then he called Vanessa. It went to voicemail.

Then he called Angie Patterson. 'I wanted to thank you again for your help tonight, but I have another question, if you don't mind.'

'Sure, Harry. Hold on though, I'm just giving my cat some food. He's always hungry before bed.'

'What's his name?' *Please don't be called Harry.*

'Alice Cooper.'

Harry was silent for a moment. 'Great. I just wanted you to remind me of the names of the kids who were left behind when their father shot himself.'

'Michael Reynolds. And his sister Dee. Well,

Doreen was her name but everybody called her Dee. They were moved into foster care and the social work department changed their names and their whole identities. I never saw Dee again for a long time.'

'You met her?'

'Yes. I was down in Edinburgh for the festival years ago and a woman came up to me and introduced herself. It was Dee. She recognised me right away. She said she missed me all those years, but the social workers took her away. She had started a new life and was even engaged.'

'Do you know what her fiancé's name was?'

'I can't remember his last name, but his first name was Vince.'

THIRTY-TWO

Rain fell hard throughout the night and Harry tossed and turned, thinking about Vince Dubois. He'd told DI Barrett from Inverness that he needed to post uniforms throughout the hotel, just to make sure everybody felt safe, even though the threat was over. People were still shaken.

'Why did he shoot the steward?' Alex had asked him. She called him when she got back to her room.

'Collateral damage. He got in the way. It's why he left the other two women alive; he just wanted Sharon Gallagher, and he got her. Making her up to look like Marie was just him playing for time. He was showing us he was in control.'

'Love's a strange thing.'

He'd slept fitfully, glad to see the sun coming in

through his bedroom window. He got up, showered and dressed and tried calling Vanessa again, hanging up when he got the voicemail. He didn't want to sound desperate. Maybe he'd just leave it until he got back home. He doubted she wanted to hear from him but maybe Alex was right, and the whole *putting all your stuff in a box* was the ice breaker she was looking for.

He put on the TV while he got his shoes on and saw the report on BBC Scotland about the killer who had savagely killed a newly-wed couple in the Highlands, as well as several other people.

Then he put his jacket on and it hit him.

He walked along to Alex's door but there was no answer. Downstairs, she was having a coffee, talking to DS Evans.

'Where's your boss?' he asked Evans.

'He'll be down shortly,' he said.

'What's the hurry, sir?'

'We want to get down the road, that's all.'

Dunbar appeared. 'Good result, Harry.'

'I just wish we had caught him rather than found him after he'd taken his own life.'

'Aye, well, at least he's no longer a threat.' He shook Harry's hand. 'I hope to see you again, pal. Safe journey home.'

'You too.' Harry and Alex were grabbing coffee when Gallagher came into the room, looking haggard.

'I appreciate all you did for us,' McNeil,' he said. 'That bastard fooled us all. It's just as well he took his own life.'

Harry took a sip of his coffee. 'You didn't tell us you had family up here, Mr Gallagher.'

The older man didn't say anything for a moment. '*Had* being the operative word. None of them live round here anymore.'

'Were they at the wedding?'

Gallagher shook his head. 'They were invited, but they didn't come.'

'I can imagine how hard it would have been for them.'

Alex looked at Harry, puzzlement on her face.

'People have long memories round here. I don't think they would have been welcomed.'

'We know all about the case,' Alex said.

Harry sipped more coffee. 'I stayed up late, playing around on the internet. Doing some research. And you know how one link leads to another. And I found out that the teacher who that person told us about, the one who murdered the two boys, was your brother. Edwin Gallagher.'

'Who told you about that?' Gallagher said, his face going red.

'It doesn't matter who told me, it's public knowledge.'

'And Mr Reynolds, the man who was the accused, might have gone down in history as a child killer, if your brother said or did nothing more. He was going to get away with it, but he couldn't help himself and he got caught. Then he decided to hang himself.'

'He was ill,' Gallagher said. 'He couldn't help himself.'

'A man killed his wife and took his own life because he couldn't stand the shame. They lived in the lodge house on the estate next to this one. Did you know that when you bought the place?'

'Of course I did. I was going to have the place razed to the ground.'

'Eradicate the memories? But here's what I think; I think that Vince Dubois used to be Michael Reynolds. He wanted to get back at your family so he killed your daughters and he killed Marie's new husband. I think Vince took a chance and started dating Marie. It was a risk, but he knew everything there was to know about her. He worked in computers after all. He got lucky when she went out with him, but she dumped him for Duncan Randall. That was just over a year ago, wasn't it? Despite you telling us otherwise. I think Marie saw thirty coming and she didn't want to be left on the shelf, and let's face it, Duncan was a good catch. Then somehow, Vince got invited to the wedding. Do you know how he got invited?'

Gallagher tried to look bored. 'No, I don't.'

'Did you know he used to date your wife as well as your daughter?'

Gallagher looked at Harry like he wanted to smack him. The cockiness had left him now. 'How the hell did you find that out?'

'I overheard Claire Blyth talking to your wife about Vince. Not nosing, you understand, but I'm not deaf either.'

'Anne obviously had a life before she met me.'

'She's only a couple of years older than Marie and you're what, sixty?'

'Fifty-five. Plenty of men have younger wives.'

'Did she tell you about Vince Dubois before you married her?' Alex asked.

'She didn't go into specifics.'

'It must have hacked you off to see him come to the wedding. Knowing he had been with both your wife and your daughter.'

'Just what is it exactly that you're getting at here, McNeil?'

Harry drank more coffee. 'I think that after young Michael Reynolds witnessed his father shooting himself after he'd killed his mother, he and his sister were taken away into foster care. They were then given a new name. I think that Michael Reynolds became Vince Dubois, and that he targeted your family. He was just waiting for the day when he could kill your daughters. Make you feel the pain that he'd felt all those years ago. I think you arranged for Angus McPhee, the lead steward, to keep his eyes and ears peeled, and then somehow, McPhee saw Vince and took him to the apartment. Where you killed him or had him killed. Not knowing he had already killed Marie and Duncan.'

Gallagher suddenly looked a lot more than his fifty-five years. 'This is just a story, isn't it?'

'I prefer to call it a working theory.'

'You couldn't be more wrong. Vince wasn't Michael Reynolds. He was just some jealous lowlife who got mad at my daughter because he thought it should be him getting married up here. But anyway, I'm heading off home now. The funeral director will take care of my daughters.'

'How can you be so sure Vince isn't Michael Reynolds?'

Gallagher turned briefly before leaving the room. 'I just am.'

Harry grabbed some toast.

'You really believe that Michael was Vince, don't you?' Alex said, pouring more coffee.

'It was just an idea I bounced about inside my head last night.'

DI Burnett came in and found Harry. 'It was good working with you, sir.'

'We're going home, now things are at an end. I'll make sure I send your Super a copy of my report and so will DS Maxwell.'

'Thank you, sir. Good working with you both.'

Harry watched as Gallagher's car drove him away from the hotel.

'Must be nice, having a private jet take you home,' Alex said.

'Him and Terence Randall. Jesus, they must both be worth a fortune.'

Just then Randall came in, looking for coffee.

'I thought they had lackeys for doing that?' Alex said.

'Probably back home, but this started out as a wedding remember?'

'True.'

Harry stood up and walked over to the man. 'I'm not going to ask you how you're feeling this morning, sir, because I can't imagine what you've gone through. I just wanted to say, if you ever need me for anything, give me a shout. I know we're from Edinburgh, but all the same.'

'That's very decent of you. Harry, isn't it?'

'It is, sir.'

'Call me Terry. I appreciate your words, Harry. My wife is going to be devastated.'

'I know. Are you going back home soon?'

'My jet just landed, so I'm going to get packed then I'll be flying home in a little while. I appreciate everything you did to try and find my son.'

The men shook hands and Harry sat back down. 'Poor bastard. I don't know how he's still standing.'

Harry was back up in his room, getting the last of his stuff together when he had a thought. He walked along to Alex's room.

'Now who's desperate?' she said.

'I want to run something by you,' he said, walking past her into the room.

'Well, my door's always open,' she said, closing it behind them. 'Not always, you understand, but most—'

'Where's the shotgun?'

'What?'

'The shotgun that Vince used to kill everybody?'

'He obviously dumped it,' Alex said, all humour gone now.

'It doesn't make sense, Alex. What if he had encountered one of the other stewards? He'd already proven that he wouldn't hesitate to kill. He shot the steward who had been with the girls. He wouldn't want to be stopped, not before he got to that apartment to kill himself. He was too much in control. That wouldn't have gone down well with him. How would he know those stewards weren't out there with their own shotguns.'

'Maybe he dumped it close by,' she said.

'No. Something's not right here. I don't think this is over. Get your bags ready, quickly. I'm going to speak to somebody.'

THIRTY-THREE

'I called my wife,' Terence Randall said as he stood up in the private jet. They had touched down at Edinburgh airport a few minutes ago and taxied to an apron reserved for the private jets. 'She's beside herself just now but says if there's any chance that there's some other bastard out there that killed our little boy, then you have everything at your disposal.'

'You've done more than enough by flying us down to Edinburgh, Terry,' Harry said.

'Gallagher didn't want to listen, did he?'

'I think he thinks people will blame him for all of this. Better to have it that a jealous ex-lover killed them all.'

'Are you going to tell me what the result of the phone call is that you made on the plane?'

'I can't go into too much detail, but members of my

team reached out to social services and it took a kick up the arse from the chief constable himself, but all they would confirm was, Michael Reynolds did *not* become Vince Dubois.'

'Somebody set him up. Bastard. Do you know who?'

'I have an idea. If I'm wrong, then it's back to the beginning.'

'Good luck, son.'

They left the plane and saw the waiting unmarked car. Karen Shiels got out and came to greet them.

'Good to see you again, sir.'

'You too, Karen. Let us put the bags in the car and we can get going.'

'I hear you did some good work up there, Alex,' Karen said.

'I was just Mr Laurel to his Mr Hardy.'

DC Simon Gregg was sitting in the back. 'Welcome back. How was that wee hooly compared to a weekend break in Blackpool?' he said, grinning.

'Definitely Blackpool next time,' Alex said, as Karen sped off.

'You know where you're going?' Harry asked.

'We've already driven past it, sir.' She looked at him. 'I wish we could have backup there as well. Considering there's a firearm involved.'

'Our careers are on the line here. In fact, I'm quite

happy for you to drop me off and you lot leave. I'll take the can for this.'

The other three detectives looked at him.

'Are you daft?' Alex said. 'If I get the boot for doing this, I'm going backpacking round the world. Screw them putting me in some other crappy department. What say you, Simon?'

'We're a team here, boss. We're all going.'

'I appreciate that. But I won't put any of you in danger.'

'Is he a big bastard?'

'He is.'

Gregg grinned. 'Magic. The bigger the better. Just point the way.'

Fifteen minutes later, they were driving slowly along the street they were looking for.

'You sure he touched down already?' Harry asked.

'Half an hour before you did,' Karen said.

'They had to change our flight plans or something,' Alex said. 'Plus, Randall's jet had to be refuelled. That's why he had a head start.'

They looked at the house they wanted, with the big wooden gate across the driveway.

Harry turned to look at them all. 'This is the last chance. I'm working on a hunch here, and if I'm wrong, then we'll all be mopping floors somewhere.'

'Then let's get the buckets ready,' Alex said, opening the car door. The others got out.

'Simon, walk past the gate and look over it. You're six foot six, so it should be easy for you.'

Gregg walked over to the gate and peered over. He turned round and gave the thumbs-up; the Range Rover was parked inside.

'Okay, round the back,' Harry ordered. Gregg and Karen took off running.

'I'm going to climb—' Harry started to say but Alex was up and over the gate before he could say another word and the wooden door beside the gate opened.

'You going to stand there all day?' she said. He quickly entered and they sprinted to the front door. It was ajar.

They both took out their extendable batons. 'Seems a bit ineffective against a sawn-off,' Alex said, but they pushed the door gently and it swung in on well-oiled hinges.

The house was a modern design. Big windows in the living room, and the same with the kitchen which was an open-plan extension of the living room.

Simon Gregg was standing outside with Karen, trying the door handle so Alex unlocked the door and opened it.

'This is Broderick Gallagher's place?' Karen said. 'Must be nice, being able to live here.'

'He's already spoken for,' Alex said. They kept their voices low.

The ground floor was empty. No signs of life.

'I'm counting on them not wanting to go out gallivanting after what's happened to his kids,' Harry said in a whisper, feeling his pension flush down the toilet.

'I know I wouldn't be,' Karen said.

They climbed the white marble stairs to the upper level and they could all smell it when they got to the top.

The master bedroom had double doors and they were both wide open.

Broderick Gallagher lay on his back on the huge bed, his front a dark red from the shotgun blast.

There was nobody else in the house.

'Jesus,' Karen said.

'That's nothing compared to what the killer did to some of the others,' Alex said.

'Where's the wife and the little boy?' Gregg said.

'I'm not sure.' A thought struck Harry. 'Karen, can you and Simon take care of this? Call it in?'

'Yes, of course, sir.'

'I can think of one more place but we're going to need backup this time. If I'm right though, we're going to have to go in stealthily, not gung ho. There's a wee boy in the middle of this.'

'I know. Let's go now,' Alex said.

Before they left, Harry told them where they were going, and that he needed somebody to make a phone call. He thought he knew where the killer was, he just didn't know exactly where.

THIRTY-FOUR

The entrance was grand, Harry had to admit. It was somewhere he could get used to living. The old Donaldson's children's school.

'They housed prisoners of war here, during the second world war, I think,' Harry said to Alex as they climbed the wide, stone steps.

'I'll keep that in the back of my mind the next time I'm at a pub quiz.'

'You're sure she told you there's nobody else in the other apartments?'

'Yes. I spoke to Kerry Hamilton herself and she says that was the only one. They're sold but the keys to the others haven't been handed over yet.'

The two members of the firearms team were right behind them.

'What's the plan, Harry? Blow the door off its

hinges? Have the entry team blast their way in?' Alex asked.

He shook his head. 'I'm just going to knock on the door. If they don't answer, the negotiator will call. No answer and the entry team go in. Hard.'

They walked along to the front door of the apartment and an armed officer stood on either side. Harry raised his hand to knock but Alex put up a hand to stop him.

'Nobody else here,' she whispered, then gently reached down for the door handle and pushed down. 'So why lock the door?'

'You were obviously brought up in the country.'

The door opened.

Harry had told the armed team that a toddler could be in here and to be extra careful. They both looked so wired up at that moment, Harry was surprised they didn't just go in guns blazing anyway.

He pushed the door in further and walked into the luxury apartment. The carpets were thick and they didn't hear anything at first, but then they heard a little boy's voice. Then he was crying.

'You were right,' Alex said.

They made it along to the living room. The door was ajar. Harry gently pushed it.

'Come in, Harry,' Claire Blythe said.

'Hello again, Dee,' he said, keeping his hands in sight. 'It *is* Dee Reynolds, isn't it?'

She smiled. 'Not for a long time.'

The further he got into the room, the more he could see they had walked into a trap.

There was a man sitting at a dining table, with a woman opposite him. He was pointing a shotgun at her. Anne Gallagher. The wall was made up of glass doors that led out onto a terrace, with the peaked rooftops behind it, giving it a secluded feel.

'We meet again, Gus,' Alex said.

Angus McPhee smiled at them. 'Sit down on those chairs across there and if you do something stupid, I'll blow her away.'

The two detectives sat down. 'Good job faking your own death,' Harry said. 'Since you all dress the same, it was easy to leave your wallet behind. Were you going to go back to using your old name, Michael?'

'I left Michael Reynolds behind a long time ago. Time for a wee change.' He kept the shotgun steady on Anne.

Rory sat on the front of the large settee with Claire behind him and a cushion in between them.

'I have one of those,' she said, nodding to her brother's shotgun. 'I don't need to tell you how unhappy I'll be if you do something silly like try to rush either of us.'

'It doesn't have to be like this, Claire,' Alex said. 'I

mean, you wouldn't want to harm a little boy, would you? You punished Broderick Gallagher already, so why don't you just let Rory go?'

'I don't think so. This is the final phase.'

Harry looked at McPhee. 'You should have left the shotgun with Vince Dubois' corpse. The gun not being there made me question everything. Up until that point, I thought Dubois was actually Michael Reynolds, that he had killed the Gallagher girls because of what Broderick's brother had done fifteen years ago. I almost got it right.'

McPhee smiled. 'Almost. Yes, we did that because of what that scumbag did to our parents. He knew his brother was guilty, but he had to have the finger pointed at my dad, just because my dad was one of the other football coaches. Gallagher had his reporters hound my dad, until he couldn't take it anymore. He knew he was being framed and would end up in prison. You of all people should know what they do to child killers inside.'

'I'm sorry your dad had to endure that, but killing Gallagher's wife and son won't bring him back.'

McPhee laughed. 'No, it won't, but it will give us satisfaction.'

Alex looked at Claire. 'That was you in Vince's house when our colleagues came round, wasn't it?'

'Yes. I just made up the first thing that came into my mind.'

'Instead of saying you were his girlfriend, which might have posed more questions. This way, we're chasing our heels looking for a phantom sister.'

Harry looked at McPhee. 'Why don't you just walk out of here and leave Claire, Mrs Gallagher and Rory with us? You can still get away. We came here alone.'

'Enough!' McPhee roared. Young Rory started crying and slipped off the settee and started running towards his mother. McPhee jumped up from the table.

And swung the shotgun at the little boy.

THIRTY-FIVE

Later on, Harry would replay this event, over and over, and in some of the replays, the shotgun blast killed him instantly, and the thought gave him nightmares.

In his twenty years as a police officer, he'd been threatened and assaulted, and had walked away from every one of those attacks. As he jumped up off the chair, he didn't think he was going to walk away from this one, but it was his instinct that propelled him across the few feet to grab Rory.

It seemed that several things happened at once; Alex was also on her feet, and she threw herself at the young woman, and then they were both flying over the settee that was tipping backwards. Her hand reached for the shotgun and pushed it upwards and it discharged into the ceiling. As they crashed to the floor, the shotgun slipped from Claire's hand and Alex punched the woman on the jaw, knocking her out.

Harry grabbed Rory and shielded him with his body, hoping the shotgun blast would hit his back and not the little boy. He didn't have time to think about dying, but he held on to the toddler, and for a split second, it reminded him of the days when he hugged his own son, Chance. Harry tensed in that moment, waiting for the pain.

As he threw himself down, still covering Rory, the first marksman's bullet cracked through the double-glazed door, deviating from its course slightly. The bullet hit Angus McPhee in the back of the head, but with the glass now shattering into a million pieces, the second one hit the target, behind McPhee's left ear, entering his brain and switching everything off. His trigger finger didn't get the message to pull the trigger and the shotgun fell silently with McPhee to the floor.

Anne Gallagher jumped up and screamed as more marksmen rushed into the living room.

Harry rolled over and Anne grabbed her now hysterical little boy.

Now it was over.

THIRTY-SIX

'You still haven't moved those boxes,' Alex said, coming in with the Chinese food. She put the bags on the little dining table by the window overlooking the bowling club.

'I've been busy,' Harry said, putting some plates down.

Alex smiled. She knew Harry was delaying emptying them as that would mean this business with Vanessa calling it a day was final. If she took him back, the boxes were already packed. It had been a week since they were up in the Highlands and she still hadn't called Harry.

Harry brought two bottles of beer from the kitchen and sat down opposite her.

'Now we've got matching commendations, we should put them in a frame,' she said.

'Mine will go in a drawer with all the other commendations.'

'Oh, look at you. How many do you have?'

'A few. To me, they're bits of paper, waiting to spring into action should I ever run out of toilet roll. To you, it means that somebody noticed your dedication and bravery.'

'I didn't think about it. I just saw that wee boy and that bitch had a gun.'

'Not everybody would have made that call.'

He looked down at the bowlers on the bowling green, having fun. It was a nice, warm evening, a time to enjoy being alive. He looked over to Vanessa's house, across the road and up the hill a bit. He wondered what she was doing, but then stopped himself. It wasn't healthy. She had made the choice and now he would have to work his life around it.

'I'm meeting Angie Patterson for a drink tomorrow,' Alex said. 'She got the job at the mortuary. She called me a little while ago.' She looked at Harry. 'Did you put in a good word for her?'

Harry made a face. 'I just told Angie there was an opening after Gus Weaver retired. I didn't make a call.'

'Liar. But it was very nice of you. I'm sure she'll appreciate it.'

'I deny all knowledge.' In fact, he had spoken to Jeni Bridge about the woman helping crack the case and it was Jeni who had put in a good word with Leo Chester, head pathologist.

'You should come along and have a drink with us.'

'Nah. You don't want me there.'

'You're right; I don't. But she does. *Bring Harry along*, she said. Please. She doesn't feel confident to ask you out herself, so she's doing it through me.'

'I'm not interested, Sergeant Maxwell.'

She laughed. 'You're so cute. Pretending you're not interested in women.'

'I never said that,' Harry said, washing some sweet and sour chicken down with the beer. 'I said I'm not interested in *that* woman.'

'Just one drink, Harry. A quick beer. She just wants to thank you.'

Harry shook his head and made a noise. 'Okay, but just one. I mean it. On a professional level, too.'

'Of course. Just one.' She clinked bottles with Harry and smiled. 'Just the one.'

AFTERWORD

I would like to thank my team of readers as always; Louise Unsworth Murphy, Wendy Haines, Julie Stott, Fiona and Adrian Jackson, Jeni Bridge, Michelle Barragan, Evelyn Bell, Merrill Astill Blount, Vanessa Kerrs, Bejay Roles and Barbara Bartley.

I would like to thank my wife Debbie who entertains the dogs, giving me time to write. And to my daughters Stephanie and Samantha.

I would also like to thank Charlie Wilson, my new editor. I appreciate her taking me on as a new client.

If I could ask you all a big favour; could you please leave a review on Amazon or Goodreads for me? Every one helps me to keep on writing and I greatly appreciate it.

John Carson
New York
August 2019

ABOUT THE AUTHOR

John Carson is originally from Edinburgh but now lives with his wife and family in New York State. He shares his house with four cats and two dogs.

website - johncarsonauthor.com
Facebook - JohnCarsonAuthor
Twitter - JohnCarsonBooks
Instagram - JohnCarsonAuthor

Manufactured by Amazon.ca
Bolton, ON

27699037R00143